"DO YOU FIND ME ATTRACTIVE?"

"Whenever I have the time," I said. "On the previous two occasions I've been too busy trying to stop from getting myself killed, to notice you much."

"There's nobody in here with a gun. Nothing to stop your concentration right now."

She got up from the armchair and unbuttoned her silk shirt slowly. When she took it off, she was naked from the waist up. Her breasts were a delicate ivory color; full, firm, with no sag at all. The coral-colored nipples stood erect, like some kind of dual challenge.

"I have the strangest feeling that I'm about to make you change your mind. . . ."

Other SIGNET Titles by Carter Brown

- ☐ AND THE UNDEAD SING (#T5864—75¢)
- ☐ THE ANGRY AMAZONS (#T5133—75¢)
- ☐ THE BLONDE (#T4883—75¢)
- ☐ BLONDE ON A BROOMSTICK (#T4936—75¢)
- ☐ THE BOMBSHELL (#T5089—75¢)
- ☐ CATCH ME A PHOENIX (#T5910—75¢)
- ☐ THE CLOWN (#T5206—75¢)
- ☐ THE DANCE OF DEATH (#T5278—75¢)
- ☐ THE DESIRED (#T5985—75¢)
- ☐ DIE ANYTIME AFTER TUESDAY (#T5175—75¢)
- ☐ THE DREAM IS DEADLY (#T5272—75¢)
- ☐ GRAVES I DIG (#T5271—75¢)
- ☐ THE INVISIBLE FLAMINI (#T4854—75¢)
- ☐ THE JADE-EYED JUNGLE (#T5167—75¢)
- ☐ THE MASTER (#T5363—75¢)
- ☐ MURDER IS SO NOSTALGIC (#T5064—75¢)
- ☐ MURDER WEARS A MANTILLA (#T5275—75¢)
- ☐ THE MYOPIC MERMAID (#T5273—75¢)
- ☐ NO BLONDE IS AN ISLAND (#T5835—75¢)
- ☐ PLAY NOW . . . KILL LATER (#T5013—75¢)
- ☐ THE PORNBROKER (#T5155—75¢)
- ☐ THE SCARLET FLUSH (#T5276—75¢)
- ☐ THE SEVEN SIRENS (#T4908—75¢)
- ☐ THE SILKEN NIGHTMARE (#T5277—75¢)
- ☐ THE STAR-CROSSED LOVER (#T5940—75¢)
- ☐ THE STRIPPER (#T5274—75¢)
- ☐ THE WIND-UP DOLL (#T4826—75¢)
- ☐ WHEELER FORTUNE (#T5795—75¢)
- ☐ WHO KILLED DR. SEX? (#T5744—75¢)

THE NEW AMERICAN LIBRARY, INC.,
P.O. Box 999, Bergenfield, New Jersey 07621

Please send me the SIGNET BOOKS I have checked above.
I am enclosing $_____(check or money order—no
currency or C.O.D.'s). Please include the list price plus 25¢ a
copy to cover handling and mailing costs. (Prices and numbers
are subject to change without notice.)

Name_____

Address_____

City_____State_____Zip Code_____
Allow at least 3 weeks for delivery

DONAVAN

by

Carter Brown

A SIGNET BOOK

NEW AMERICAN LIBRARY

TIMES MIRROR

Published by arrangement with Alan G. Yates

SIGNET TRADEMARK REG. U.S. PAT. OFF. AND FOREIGN COUNTRIES
REGISTERED TRADEMARK—MARCA REGISTRADA
HECHO EN CHICAGO, U.S.A.

SIGNET, SIGNET CLASSICS, MENTOR, PLUME AND MERIDIAN BOOKS
are published by The New American Library, Inc.,
1301 Avenue of the Americas, New York, New York 10019

FIRST PRINTING, AUGUST, 1974

  1 2 3 4 5 6 7 8 9

PRINTED IN THE UNITED STATES OF AMERICA

CHAPTER ONE

The Bristol is one of the few remaining older hotels in New York that maintains its standards. You can still ride in one of their elevators with an almost complacent assurance that you will not be mugged on the way up. I am known at the hotel, so it is never a problem to take over their private three-bedroom suite whenever I am in New York. I also make it a practice never to travel alone because I am easily bored with my own company.

This time I had with me, as a traveling companion, Tamara Wentworth. The unlikely combination of her first and second names was undoubtedly invented by Tamara at some stage of her brief and trivial career as an exotic dancer, before the permissive society overtook her and made her career as outdated as the ballerina dress. Tamara is magnificently plump. You can get a real stimulating massage by simply rolling your head up and down the length of her torso, on either side. She has no brains, no conversation, but she is remarkably inventive where sex is concerned.

Hicks, my man, unpacked the bags as soon as we got up into the suite. The English still make the best servants in the whole world. The trick, these days, is to find one willing to become a servant. With a deft mixture of flattery and bribery, I persuaded Hicks a couple of years back that his best future lay in becoming my manservant. I promised him money, travel, and the pick of my cast-off wardrobe. Since then, he has never looked back. Admittedly our master-manservant relationship has changed somewhat since the time he started working for me, but in these days of aggressive egalitarianism it is only to be expected. I had just finished making myself a vodka and pure apple juice, when he came into the living room of the suite.

"She's having a bath," he announced. "Bleeding great mountain of foam, and it stinks of perfume." He rolled his eyes expressively. "Reminds me of that bordello in Venice you took me to one time. You remember the place? They gave you a small whip as you came in, and all the tarts had feathers stuck up their asses."

"Horse-feathers, of course," I said.

"Is that what they were?" He looked mildly interested. "She wants to know if you'd care to join her in the bath. I told her you wouldn't."

"How the hell do you know I wouldn't?"

"Look, mate," he said reasonably. "You know what would happen, don't you? You'd slip on the bleeding bathmat and probably go straight out the window. Or worse"—he chuckled coarsely—

"dive headfirst straight between her legs and finish up out of sight for the next six months!"

"You have a revolting sense of humor," I told him.

"I can't help that, can I, then?" He made himself a Scotch and water, but with no ice, of course. "What are we going to do now we're in New York, anyway?"

The phone rang and he answered it, his voice immediately changing from its natural London-cum-cockney accent to something so incredibly refined it would knock saccharin clean off the market, if you could only find some way of bottling it.

"Mr. Paul Donavan's suite," he announced, then listened for a few seconds. "May I request to whom I am speaking? . . . Hold the line please, and I shall inquire." He put his hand over the mouthpiece and winked at me. "Some bird wants to talk to you," he said. "Won't give her name. Sounds a bit of all right. All husky, like she's in heat already."

I took the phone from him and said, "Paul Donavan speaking."

"Mr. Donavan, you won't know me, but I'm a friend of Karl Madden," the feminine voice said. Hicks had been right about it. It *was* husky, kind of bubbling with unrestrained sexuality.

"What can I do for you?" I asked courteously.

"I have an urgent problem and it just won't wait," she said. "Karl says you're the only person who can possibly help me. Would you meet me thirty minutes from now?"

"Sure," I said. "Where?"

"There's a bar called the Arden on Lexington, between Fifty-seventh and Fifty-eighth."

"I'll be there," I said. "How will I recognize you?"

"Don't worry, Mr. Donavan," she said, and chuckled softly. "I'll recognize you." Then she hung up.

I put the phone down and moved back to my drink.

"Who was she?" Hicks asked hopefully.

"She didn't say, but she wants me to meet her in a bar in a half hour," I said. "Karl says I'm the only one who can help her."

"Karl who?" Hicks asked.

"Karl Madden," I told him.

His forehead wrinkled. "Do we know any Karl Madden?"

"No," I said.

"It sounds a bit dodgy to me." He shook his head slowly. "With all those bleeding millions you got, you want to be a bit careful, mate. First thing you know, you'll find yourself kidnapped, and after we've paid a bleeding great ransom, you'll turn up dead in the East River. And where will that leave me, I'd like to know? Out of a bleeding soft job, that's where!"

"We'll take the usual precautions," I said.

"Bloody hell!" he said dismally. "I was looking forward to a night off. Going to one of them sin-

gles bars and finding myself a nice bit of crack-
ling."

I checked my wristwatch. "We don't have too
much time," I said.

"All right." He gestured with his thumb in the
vague direction of the bathroom. "What about
her?"

"What about her?" I said.

"You're right." He nodded vigorously. "Spends
half her life in the bath, that tart does. What do
you think she does? Has it off with a bar of soap,
or something?"

"And change your clothes," I told him. "In that
batik shirt and silk sportcoat, you look like a re-
ject from some old Edward G. Robinson movie."

"So that's why you gave them to me!" he said
indignantly. "So I can walk around looking like
some poof?"

Hicks is around average height, and his build is
deceptive. He has thick black hair, eyes so deep a
blue they are almost black, and a nose that was
perhaps elegant before it got broken a couple of
times. A livid knife-scar—a relic from his days in
the Congo as a mercenary—runs down from one
corner of his mouth to the edge of his chin and
gives him a perpetual sneer. Just looking at him
makes a lot of adults feel distinctly nervous, and
small children usually run screaming at their first
sight of him. Put him in a short dress covered
with tinsel, put a wand in his hand, and still nobody in his right mind would ever mistake him
for a fairy.

I took a cab from the hotel to the bar, and it was just after seven P.M. when I arrived. The Arden bar was in semidarkness, and perhaps one-quarter full. I stood for a few seconds just inside the doorway, until my eyes became accustomed to the gloom, then saw the girl approaching me. She was a brunette, tall and slim, wearing a black velvet pantsuit with a white silk shirt. As she came closer, I saw she exuded an aura of confidence that bordered on arrogance.

"Mr. Donavan," she said, in a low husky voice. "You're four minutes late."

Then she turned on her heel and led the way to a corner banquette. We sat down, side by side, and a waiter arrived. The brunette already had an obviously untasted drink in front of her, so I ordered a vodka and pure apple juice for myself.

"Karl Madden sends his very best regards," the brunette said, after the waiter had gone on his way.

"That's nice," I told her. "I'd like to meet him sometime."

She chuckled, and it was a risible round. "I thought about it for a long while," she said. "How to interest the jaded and sex-surfeited palate of the rich Mr. Paul Donavan."

"How long did it take you to dream up a phrase like that?" I asked her.

"Long enough." She shrugged gently. "I know money doesn't interest you because you've got too much of it already, and I couldn't compete with all those semi-professional girls who must keep on throwing themselves at you, so the only way I figured I could get to talk with you was by awakening your curiosity."

"Okay," I said. "You've proved your point. So what do you want from me?"

She waited until the waiter had served my drink, then said, "Your help."

"For what?"

"I've done my research on you real good, Mr. Donavan," she said. "You're a fighter of lost causes."

"Don't be stupid," I said. "Sure, I'll admit there were a couple of times when—"

"A couple of times?" The sneer in her voice was painfully audible. "Tell me the name of one of the new African states where you could get off an airplane and not be put straight back onto it again?"

"Can I help it if they've all gone the wrong way?" I said defensively. "Now they're all military dictatorships, run by raving crackpots who—"

"If you want to cry," she said brutally, "please cry into your own drink, Mr. Donavan."

"All right," I said, keeping my temper with some difficulty. "So why do you want help from a born loser?"

"Because nobody else will help me. No"—she quickly corrected herself—"that's not strictly true. You're a whole mess of contradictions, Mr. Donavan. You've helped people on the extreme left, the extreme right, and sometimes in the dead center. What motivates you?"

"You're writing an article for a magazine, perhaps?" I asked doubtfully. "Or dabbling in amateur psychology? Looking for material for your Ph.D. thesis?"

"Crap!" she said energetically. "I have an urgent problem—a matter of life and death—and I desperately need your help. If I could begin to understand what motivates you, then maybe I'd know a sure way of getting you on my side."

"My father was an inventive genius," I said. "He made millions out of his patents, then left everything to me when he died. Most of his patents keep right on making money. I left college in my sophomore year because it seemed pointless, and I bummed my way around the world for another year until that seemed pointless, too. At heart I'm a sybarite but—as in all things—you've got to have contrast before you can have enjoyment. So I took up causes. Any cause that looked interesting, and where my involvement wouldn't become dull. I like sex, luxury, and excitement, in approximately that order." I smiled at her briefly. "Does that answer your goddamned impertinent question?"

"I guess it does," she said, in a small voice. "You have to be some kind of a nut!"

"You're probably right," I agreed, "and since we don't seem to be getting anyplace, you won't forget to give my warmest regards to Karl?"

I was halfway to my feet, when she grabbed my arm and pulled me back down onto the banquette again.

"Hold it," she said. "You haven't heard my proposition yet."

"I was beginning to figure I never would," I said truthfully.

"Karl Madden exists," she said. "He's in great danger because he knows too much about the real reason why—"

She stopped speaking suddenly, and her face froze as she looked at something over my right shoulder. I turned my head quickly, just in time to see the guy heading straight toward us. He was small, with sandy-colored hair, and he had a tight grin on his face. He was also holding a gun in his right hand.

I gripped the edge of the table with both hands and heaved, then grabbed hold of the brunette as the table crashed over onto its side and pulled her down onto the floor. She yelped as I landed on top of her, but she made a comfortable cushion. Appearances were deceptive, I realized. Underneath that black velvet pantsuit, her breasts were surprisingly large and firm. The sound of two shots being fired in quick succession was incredibly loud in the confined space, and then all hell seemed to break loose as people started screaming and yelling inside the bar.

There was a soft thump as something landed on the floor beside us. I looked and saw it was a gun. Then I turned my head cautiously and looked upward, and there he was, grinning down at me. His shoulders were resting on the edge of the upturned table, so his face was only about three feet away from mine. It was a momentarily unnerving experience until I realized that whatever it was his fixed gaze was staring at, it had nothing to do with this world.

I got back up onto my feet, without hurrying, and the reason why the guy with the sandy-colored hair had lost interest became apparent. The back of his head had been blown off. About all that was left of it was a pink-and-red bloody mess. I yanked the brunette onto her feet and gave her a general push in the direction of the door. The bar had cleared very quickly. We were just about the only ones left inside, apart from a couple of gray-faced waiters who had taken refuge in back of the bar itself. So we got out onto the street and started walking briskly.

"As you were saying?" I said brightly.

"I guess you saved my life," the brunette said, in a shaking voice.

"Not necessarily," I told her. "It depends which one of us he wanted to kill."

"It was me, all right," she said. "I know it! And it means they were following me." She stopped suddenly. "I have to let Karl know immediately. We thought I was in the clear, and it'll be dangerous for him—even more dangerous!—now they know about me."

"I'll come with you," I said generously.

"No." She shook her head vehemently. "I have to see Karl first. I'll contact you again, later. At the hotel."

She walked to the edge of the sidewalk, raised her right hand, and an empty cab stopped right beside her about five seconds later. I hate people who can do that.

"Wait a minute," I said, as she got into the cab. "I don't even know your name."

"Moira," she said. "Moira Stevens."

Then she was gone. I waited until another cab passed me, heading in the same direction, with the only passenger a sinister-looking character with a busted nose and a scar running down one side of his chin, then I went back to the hotel.

CHAPTER TWO

"There was this man who called you," Tamara said in a reproachful voice. "I had to get out of the bath to answer the phone."

"I know it was a great sacrifice," I said. "I can't thank you enough."

Tamara is, in many ways, an old-fashioned girl. Certainly her taste in lingerie shows a definite nostalgia for the thirties. She was wearing a black bra, made entirely from fine lace, and the dusty-pink of her large nipples showing through the lace made a piquant color contrast. Everything else was black, too—panties, garters, silk stockings, and mules on her feet complete with pompoms on the instep. It's very difficult to think about anything other than sex when you're with Tamara, because you know she never thinks about anything else, either.

"His name is Pace," she said. "Everard Pace. Or maybe he was making a joke?"

"Ever hard?" I shook my head. "I don't think so."

"He sounded annoyed when I told him you

were out. He's going to call back. It's urgent he sees you, he said."

"Fine," I said.

"Darling Paul." She blinked slowly, and there was a desolate look in her large brown eyes. "Are you getting bored with me?"

"Definitely not," I said. "Whatever makes you think that?"

"You keep on rejecting me." She caught her full lower lip between her teeth and held it there for a few seconds. "Last night, on the airplane, you wouldn't do it."

"Flying makes me nervous," I said. "Besides, there were all those other people around."

"In the middle of the night," she said bleakly, "who would have noticed if we both went to the same toilet? I told you there would be plenty of room if I sat on the washbasin and put my legs around your neck, but you still wouldn't."

"Flying makes me nervous," I said, "and I was worried. Suppose we hit an air pocket right in the middle of it and suddenly dropped a couple of hundred feet? It would probably mean we'd be kind of welded together for the rest of our lives."

"Earlier this evening I sent you an invitation to join me in the bath, and you never came." Her lower lip pouted ominously. "That's twice you've rejected me inside twenty-four hours! There's something very wrong here, Paul. You don't think I'm getting thin, or something?"

"Something came up so I had to go out," I said. "You know that."

There was the sound of a key being inserted in the lock, and Tamara's face flushed.

"Maybe we should go and do it in Times Square?" she snarled. "We'd get more privacy there!"

"What's wrong with later tonight?" I asked reasonably.

"Nothing," she said. "So long as you don't forget again."

She turned on her heel and stomped out of the room, her large, beautifully rounded buttocks bouncing wildly as she went. Hicks walked into the room, closed the door in back of him carefully, then headed straight toward the bar.

"You can make me a vodka and pure apple juice," I said. "I never did get the chance to finish my drink in that bar."

"I was glad you knocked over the table," he said. "I wouldn't have known, otherwise."

"He had a gun in his hand," I said.

"Not when he went past me, he didn't. He was walking toward the bar, then he suddenly changed direction at the last moment and headed straight toward you."

"It was good shooting," I said.

"I like the double-action trigger on the Smith and Wesson," he said. "Saves that vital second, like they say."

"How about the girl?" I asked him.

He handed me my drink, then picked up his own. "I must be getting bloody old!" he said disgustedly. "I lost her. She got out at a red light and took off down Second Avenue. By the time my cab reached the lights and I'd paid the bleeding driver, she'd disappeared."

"She's supposed to be contacting me again," I said.

"Don't go and have another drink with her in a bar," he pleaded, "or they'll start calling me the killer that stalks New York by night!"

The phone rang and he answered it, adopting his phony, incredibly refined accent. He listened for a few seconds, then put his hand over the mouthpiece. "Some git called Pace is downstairs. Wants to see you right away."

"Tell him to come on up," I said.

He did as I said, then hung up the phone. "Everard Pace?" he said suspiciously. "You think he's taking the mickey out of me or something?"

"No," I said wearily.

"You know him?"

"I know of him," I said. "He's the reason we're here in New York."

"Oh?" He shrugged expressively. "Well, don't take me into your confidence, will you? I mean, I'm only the poor sod who has to worry about saving your life three times a bleeding week!"

"All will be revealed," I promised him. "Once I know what all is."

Pace arrived a couple of minutes later, and Hicks put his best butler's foot forward as he ushered him into the living room. He was someplace in his mid-forties, I figured, with close-cropped black hair going gray around the edges. His pale blue eyes were deepset either side of a prominent nose, and the deep tan gave the skin of his face a weathered look. He was about six feet, with no obvious fat, and the clipped mustache on his upper lip gave him a military appearance.

"Mr. Donavan," he said, in the kind of British accent that doesn't quite ring true. "I'm Everard Pace."

"Would you like a drink?" I said politely.

"Why not?" He looked at Hicks. "Whiskey, water, and none of your American ice."

"Yes, sir," Hicks said woodenly. "Would you prefer some British ice instead? Or we do have a little left of the Icelandic ice. Vintage '67, as I remember."

"Never mind, Hicks," I said quickly. "I'll make Mr. Pace's drink myself."

"Yes, sir. Will that be all, sir?"

"I think so," I said.

"Then I'll go and run madame's bath for her," he said, and started toward the door.

"She's just had a bath," I snarled.

"But that was at least fifteen minutes ago, sir!" he said triumphantly, the moment before he disappeared out of sight.

I moved around in back of the bar and decided to ignore the blank look on Pace's face as I made him a drink.

"You obviously received our message, or you wouldn't be here in New York right now," he said.

"Right," I told him, and pushed his drink across the bartop toward him.

"Cheers!" He lifted the glass and drank deeply. "I'd prefer to keep names out of this conversation, if you don't mind, Donavan."

"I don't mind at all," I told him.

"Not that I don't trust you," he said generously. "But everyone seems to have gotten the bugging bug these days. Well"—he drank a little more, then put his glass down on the bartop—"you know whom I represent?"

"Sure," I said.

He picked up his drink again, took it with him to the nearest armchair, and settled himself comfortably.

"You don't mind if I briefly re-cap the situation?" He gave me a perfunctory smile. "Just so we're both clear about what, exactly, we're talking about."

"Go ahead," I said.

"It was a tribal situation," he said. "You decided to back the minority tribe for reasons of your own. You bought a shipment of arms and delivered them. You also gave them enough money to hire themselves a small band of mercenaries. Am I right?"

"It's very possible," I said.

"Ah!" He smiled briefly again. "I can assure you, I don't carry a personal bug, Mr. Donavan!"

"I'm glad to hear it," I said.

"The revolution failed," he went on. "To be blunt, your side lost."

"So I heard," I said.

"Not so much lost, as were bloodily massacred,"

he said. "Did you hear about that, Mr. Donavan?"

"Not in detail," I said. "Only the general out-line."

"Do you know why?" he asked softly.

"I guess you're going to tell me," I said.

He took the tip of his prominent nose between his thumb and index finger and pulled on it reflectively. "In essence, the whole shipment had been tampered with," he said. "For example, the barrels of, say, one out of every four rifles had been slightly bent. Not enough so it was apparent to the naked eye, but enough so the rifle exploded when the trigger was pulled, with unfortunate results to the poor fellow who happened to be holding it at the time. There was more. Lots more! The ammunition had been got at, a number of the grenades had been short-fused—but need I go on?"

"I get the general picture," I said.

"It caused a great deal of alarm and despondency," he said. "Your side lost their revolution, with the inevitable unhappy sequence of events. Now, frankly, Mr. Donavan, we're not overly concerned about what happens to some tribal primitives. But some of the mercenaries survived, and they are *most* unhappy about what happened." He pulled his nose again. "It affects our reputation, you see."

"I see," I said.

He finished his drink and held out the empty glass toward me. "Do you think I could possibly have another?"

"Help yourself," I said, and pushed the whiskey bottle a couple of inches further along the bartop.

His face flushed slightly, then he got up out of the armchair and came across to the bar.

"We're a professional organization," he said. "We can guarantee to supply a virtually unlimited quantity of arms, in top-class condition, almost anywhere in the world. Our reputation, up until now, has never been questioned. You see the dilemma this unfortunate situation puts us in."

"So why tell me?" I said.

"Oh come, Mr. Donavan!" He poured whiskey into his glass, then followed it with teaspoonsful of water. "You aren't that naïve. You bought the arms from us, and we know they were in perfect condition when you took delivery. You chartered your own ship to carry them to where they were to be used, and you traveled with them. You, and your bully-boy, who masquerades as your manservant. It's incredible to even think your friends tampered with them after they had taken delivery from you, because it would have been a most peculiar form of mass suicide. So the guns and the rest of it must have been tampered with while they were under your control."

"It's possible," I conceded.

"Frankly, Mr. Donavan, it worries us," he said. "We're professionals, you see, and we can't afford to have our reputation damaged in any way. But you"—he sniffed faintly—"well, not to put too fine a point on it, you're a bloody amateur. You're not in this for money or anything reasonable, just for some crazy idealistic crap of your own. That means you're unstable, you see?"

"I see," I said.

He pulled his nose again irritably, and I hoped it hurt. "The ship was an old Danish tramp," he said, "flying a Panamanian flag. The skipper was a German, the crew a motley collection of deadbeats who were only interested in collecting their bonus at the end of the voyage. But we checked them out, all the same. Our men, as you remember, supervised the loading of the shipment, and you sailed a half hour after the loading was complete. We just don't believe any crew member could have done the sabotage. It took a lot of expert knowledge, apart from anything else, and none of them had it"

"Which leaves?" I said obligingly.

"Yourself," he said. "Your man, Hicks, and your two other companions, Travers and Dryden."

"Professionals," I said. "I had them along in case we ran into any trouble during the voyage. The four of us kept a very good eye on the cargo the whole time."

"I was almost forgetting," he said. "You had a woman along with you, but then you usually do."

"Francine Delato," I said. "Francine wouldn't fool around with guns, it might chip the silver polish from her nails."

"Out of the approximately thirty mercenaries hired with your money, only five survived." He picked up his glass and swallowed another mouthful of Scotch. "Two of them are busy following their trade in another part of Africa and are reasonably philosophic about the whole thing. The other three feel differently."

"And they are?" I asked him.

"Alexei DuPlessis, Hank Sheppard, and Karl Madden," he said. "They hold you responsible for what happened." He waved one hand expansively. "We want to be fair, Mr. Donavan. If you're suddenly killed by one, or all three, of these gentlemen, it will provide a satisfactory explanation of what went wrong with the shipment, and our reputation will regain its pristine quality. On the other hand, we would like to be sure revenge is taken on the person, or persons, actually responsible. We wouldn't want a possible reoccurence. That's why we decided to apprise you of the situation."

"You're too kind, Mr. Pace," I said.

"The least we could do," he said. "Is Miss Delato with you at the moment?"

"I'm sure you know she isn't," I said.

"It occurs to me that she could be in danger," he said placidly. "One of the mercenaries might decide she could prove to be a valuable hostage, or perhaps think she could have some vital information concerning the sabotage."

"I'll keep it in mind," I said.

"Well, I should be getting along." He finished his drink in one long gulp. "I have another appointment later. Not about the same matter, you understand." He chuckled briefly. "This is with a prospective buyer. Much more straightforward."

I walked with him to the door and opened it for him. He didn't offer to shake hands, and that solved a problem for me.

"Take care, Mr. Donavan," he said.

"Everard?" I said. "It's not some kind of a joke?"

His mustache twitched sharply, then he started off down the corridor. I closed the door and walked back into the suite. Some fool must have moved a chair when I wasn't looking, because I fell over it and barked my shins painfully. I was just picking myself up off the floor, when I saw Hicks had already established himself in back of the bar and was busy making himself a drink.

"You're getting excited again, mate," he said.

"I am not getting excited!" I said tightly.

"I can tell." He sniffed disparagingly. "You always start falling over things when you get excited. Accident-prone, that's what you are."

"Nonsense!" I snarled.

"I don't blame you for getting excited, mate," he said generously. "It's something to get excited about."

"You listened, of course," I said.

"Of course." He nodded slowly. "One thing, we know where one of the three bastards is right now."

"Karl Madden," I agreed. "Right here in New York."

"The only one I know is DuPlessis," Hicks said. "I was with him in the Congo. Ripe bastard, he is! Used to keep his own private harem with him.

Five of them, all chained together, and the oldest was maybe sixteen, at most. One time we had to pull out real fast and there was no chance of him taking his harem along. Only DuPlessis hated leaving anything usable behind, so he slit their throats and left them, still all chained together. The first time I see his ugly face again, I'm going to start shooting."

"If he doesn't see you first," I said.

"That's right," he said morosely, "cheer me up! What are we going to do now, mate? Dig a hole and pull it in after us?"

"There's no point in going to ground," I told him. "They'd find us anyway."

"They can find us here without even trying," he said. "Both Madden and that Pace bastard already have."

"We've got to find them first," I said. "Especially Travers and Dryden. Not forgetting Francine, either."

"You're right," he said. "Why don't we move out to your house in Connecticut?"

"Turn it into a fortress and sit around growing old while we wait?" I said.

"I mean, there's no bloody point in going after them with a couple of handguns," he said. "We need some weight."

"You're right," I said. "You want to go out to the house and get some?"

"Tonight?" he said dismally.

"I guess it can wait until morning," I said.

"You've got your Smith and Wesson, and I've got the Walther."

"So I might have a night off, mate?" he asked. "I'll rent a car in the morning and go out to Connecticut and pick up some of the necessary. Should be back by midday. All right?"

"Why not?" I said.

"Don't do anything stupid while I'm gone," he said sternly. "I mean like going out on your own, or tripping over that tart in the bedroom and breaking your bloody arm. We're going to need each other, mate!"

CHAPTER THREE

There were four locks on the outer door of the suite. After the waiter had cleared away the remains of our dinner, I locked two of them, leaving two unlocked. It's guaranteed to drive any lock-picker out of his mind. Every time he picks four locks, he relocks two of them. Then I went back into the living room. Tamara had gone to the bedroom, I presumed, and I had time for a Napoleon brandy nightcap before I joined her. It had been tacitly agreed between us that I would help her enact her favorite sexual fantasy, as a kind of atonement for refusing her favors on the airplane the previous night.

I guess most people have their own special sexual fantasies, and Tamara was certainly no exception. Hers made her the abject slave of a cruel and vicious master, whom she had somehow displeased. As a punishment, she was forced to lie down on a bed, naked, her face buried in a cushion, and tremblingly await his retribution. When it actually came to the point, I always found a couple of hefty slaps across her ripe bottom were adequate, but Tamara got all her kicks out of the anticipation.

So I poured the brandy into a snifter and settled down in an armchair to enjoy it. The phone rang when I was about halfway through the drink.

"Mr. Donavan?" The voice was subdued, husky, and familiar.

"Moira Stevens?"

"Karl Madden wants to see you, and he says it won't wait."

"I could get killed," I told her.

"Not this time," she said. "No more meetings in public. Just the both of you in a very well-protected place."

"Like where?"

"A penthouse on the East River," she said. "Nobody gets in unless Karl wants them to." Then she gave me the address.

"Will you be there?" I asked her.

"Does it matter?"

"I want you there," I said. "I want you to open the door to me, or I don't come."

"I didn't realize my fatal charms had impressed you that much, Mr. Donavan," she said dryly.

"I want a hostage to keep me company while I'm there," I said. "If anything nasty even looks like happening, you'll die first."

"You bastard!" There was a silence that lasted around five seconds, and her voice was impersonal when she spoke again. "I'll be there," she said, then hung up.

I put a fresh magazine into the Walther PP, pushed the safety down and pulled the slide to the back, then released it, before I pushed the safety back up into the off position. Now the gun would fire on double action by pulling through on the trigger, and as Hicks said, it's saving that extra second that can make a hell of a lot of difference. Then I put the gun into a belt holster around my waist and finished my brandy. I was almost to the door when I suddenly remembered Tamara. It seemed somehow unfair to just leave her without any kind of good-bye, so I retraced my steps to the bedroom.

As she heard me enter the room, Tamara's whole body twitched with anticipation. Her face was buried in the cushion, her long blond hair spread like a fan across her shoulders. The concentric spheres of her bottom gleamed whitely in the soft light from the shaded table lamp, and her legs were spread wide apart, revealing a fascinating fringe of soft, curling pubic hair between the tops of her legs. I gave the right cheek a resounding slap, and she shrieked in mock terror while it was still quivering. Then I gave the left cheek an equally resounding slap.

"Mercy!" she whispered. "Please, Master! I can't stand any more pain!"

Tamara's trouble is that her fantasies have no literary qualities at all. I have seriously considered hiring a scriptwriter to provide her with some more interesting dialogue, but I suspect she wouldn't be much good at remembering lines, either.

"Even the brutal beating I have just given you is far less than you deserve, slave," I said solemnly. "Even now, my head eunuch is busy plaiting a horsewhip with small steel barbs. When it is ready, I shall return and flay the skin from your body with it."

"Oh, no, not that!" Her torso writhed in ecstasy.

"Think about the whip plaited with small steel barbs," I said. "When I return with it, your agony will be unbearable!"

I walked out of the room and closed the door gently on her happy whimpering sounds. With any reasonable luck, I hoped the new fantasy might keep her going until I got back.

The apartment block was in the Eighties, elegant and right up against the East River. I rode the slow-moving elevator to the eighteenth floor with an elevator man who looked old enough to be Whistler's father. The door opened almost before I had removed my thumb from the button, and Moira Stevens stood there. Her black hair had been brushed straight back, so it sat sleek on her head, and she was wearing a full-length gown of thin black silk that fit her like a sheath all the way down to her knees and was semi-transparent. Her full breasts were outlined in startling detail, and her nipples dimpled the silk. The aura of arrogance was back in the way she held her head, and in the disdainful curve of her full lower lip. For a fleeting moment there, I wondered if I should have ordered two of those horsewhips plaited with small steel barbs from my head eunuch.

"I thought you might need reassurance, Mr. Donavan," she said. "As you can see, there are no concealed weapons."

"I wouldn't say that," I demurred.

"Are you always that obvious?" She sighed. "But then, I guess with your money you don't have to worry."

She turned her back on me and started walking, leaving me to close the front door. I caught up with her at the far side of the wide-tiled entrance hall.

"Karl is waiting for you in the library," she said. "You want me to go in first?"

"Please," I said politely.

She opened the door and walked into the room, with me following right in back of her. It was a library, just as she had said—a pleasant, rectangular-shaped room with book-lined walls. Sitting behind a leather-topped desk was a man who had to be Karl Madden. Apart from the three of us, the room was empty. I made very sure of that. There was no place for anybody to hide.

Madden was a big guy, and his suit didn't hide the muscles that bulged just about everyplace. Thick, black, curly hair had receded about halfway across the top of his head, and a luxuriant mustache tried hard to make up for the deficit. His eyes were a gelid blue, set deep in a weatherbeaten face, the color of unpolished mahogany. His mouth was large, and his lips were thick and wet-looking.

"Sit down, Mr. Donavan," he said, in a deep bass voice.

I sat down in the nearest leather armchair and didn't relax for a moment.

"I guess you don't need me anymore," the brunette said, in a bored tone.

"You underestimate your fatal charms," I told her, then pointed at the other leather armchair. "Sit down."

She sat down with her lips tightly compressed and glared at me murderously.

"You financed the hiring of the mercenaries, and you paid for the shipment of arms for them to fight with, Mr. Donavan," Madden said evenly. "You even delivered them yourself. But they'd been gotten at."

"So I've heard," I said.

"Thirty of us," he said, "and only five survived."

"You work in a dangerous profession, Mr. Madden," I said. "Ask any insurance company."

"We all wanted revenge," he said. "DuPlessis most of all. But then a couple of them cooled off and changed their minds. That left three of us."

"Your arithmetic is impeccable, Mr. Madden," I said.

His eyes glittered for a moment. "Don't make me change my mind, now I've come this far!" he said. "DuPlessis made elaborate plans—good, workable, elaborate plans—for you, Mr. Donavan. And now he's just about started to put them into action."

"Are you part of it?" I asked.

He shook his head slowly. "I changed my mind," he said.

"Charity?"

"Simple arithmetic," he said. "Like you said, Mr. Donavan, I'm real good at that. What would I get out of helping them to take revenge on you?"

"You tell me."

"Not too much, when I came to think about it," he said. "Especially when I came to think about you, Mr. Donavan. Dead, you wouldn't be worth anything to me. Alive?"

"Ah," I said wisely. "You're trying to sell me something, Mr. Madden?"

"I took one hell of a chance," he said. "When I ran out on them, I put my own life in as much danger as yours is right now. They want me dead before I can get to you. They've already tried a couple of times!"

"They know you know their plans," I said. "Won't they change them?"

"Sure," he said easily. "But there's one central factor that can't be altered. Everything hinges on that."

"Which is?" I asked.

"Worth a lot of money." He leaned back in his chair and stared at me coldly. "Like it or not, Mr. Donavan, when I ran out on them I'd joined forces with you as far as they were concerned. So now there's only one choice left; either they kill us, or we kill them."

"And just to cement the partnership, you want some money," I said. "How much?"

"Half million dollars," he said, without twitching.

"I don't carry that kind of cash money around with me," I told him.

"I'll take your word you'll pay," he said.

"I'm surprised at your generosity."

"It's not a lot of money, Mr. Donavan." He grinned faintly. "Not in your kind of money language."

"You can give me the information and I can still wind up dead," I said. "I'll pay you after we've gotten rid of Sheppard and DuPlessis."

The silence in the room started to sound loud while he thought about it. Moira Stevens just sat there with a bored expression on her face. I let my mind start to wander, because it was getting bored where it was right then.

"All right," Madden said finally. "You got yourself a deal."

"You're very trusting, Karl," the brunette said, in a derisive voice. "It's not like you."

"Donavan won't renege," he said confidently.

"So what are their plans?" I asked him.

"They're in no hurry to kill you," he said. "They want revenge. A bullet through the back of your head would be too quick and too easy. No fun in that! You had a girl with you on the boat, right?"

"Francine Delato," I agreed.

"They're going to grab her for bait," he said, "for the both of you. They want your guy, Hicks, too. DuPlessis was with him in the Congo and he hates him, for some reason."

"Where and when?" I asked.

"England," he said. "They checked on her movements. She's going to visit with friends in some country place. They'll grab her while she's there. After that, they plan on sending you some graphic pictures of the kind of hospitality she's enjoying. If that doesn't bring you fast, they figure on sending you something more personal, like a finger."

"Okay," I said. "I'll meet you in London in a couple of days' time."

"Where?" he asked.

"A hotel in Bayswater called the Sedan Chair," I said. "I'll book you a room." I looked at the brunette. "Two rooms?"

"Two rooms," she said, "and who pays the air fare?"

"Your good friend, Mr. Madden," I said. "With his expectations, he can afford it." I got up onto my feet. "Good-bye for now, Mr. Madden."

"We'll see you in London, Mr. Donavan," he said. "Moira will drive you back to your hotel."

"I can get a cab," I said.

"Your life is suddenly very precious to me." He grinned again. "I'd feel a lot happier if you let Moira drive you."

We rode the elevator down to the lobby, and Whistler's father looked visibly shaken when he got a full frontal view of the brunette's semi-transparent black gown. Then we went out onto

the sidewalk, and Moira Stevens unlocked the
door on the passenger's side of a beat-up Volks-
wagen.

Diagonally across the street, a black sedan pulled
out from the curb and started to move toward
us, showing no lights. I went down onto my knees
real fast, pulling the girl down with me, then
grabbed the Walther from my belt holster. There
was a staccato chatter, followed by the shrill
whining sound as bullets ricocheted from the
body of the car and off the sidewalk. The next moment the other car was past us and beginning to
accelerate. I braced my left wrist under my right,
took careful aim, and loosed off four shots. About
a hundred yards down the street, the black sedan
suddenly swerved crazily as the gas tank exploded,
then mounted the curb and came to an abrupt stop
against a lamppost. A guy got out of the driver's
side and took a couple of lurching steps forward
before he fell flat on his face.

I put my gun away, lifted the brunette back
onto her feet, bundled her into the passenger's
seat of the car, then took the keys out of her fingers. It took almost no time at all to unlock the
door on the driver's side, get behind the wheel,
and start the motor. I made a tight U-turn and
headed in the opposite direction to the burning
car.

"My God!" Moira Stevens said in a faint voice,
about four blocks later. "This is the second time
I've been with you, and it's the second time somebody's gotten killed."

"I don't think the guy who got out of the car was dead," I protested mildly; "more like confused."

"I don't think there's enough money in the whole world to make it worthwhile getting mixed up with you, Paul Donavan," she said tightly. "And don't think I'm not going to tell Karl that!"

"Have you ever met DuPlessis or Sheppard?" I asked her.

"No."

"It would be nice if one of them was the guy in the bar," I said, "because he's dead. It would also be nice if the guy who got out of the car was the other one, because I think he must have done himself some damage when the car hit the lamppost."

"Why do you think they could have been Sheppard and DuPlessis?"

"Because if they weren't," I said, with matchless logic, "who in hell were they?"

It must have been a good question, because it kept her thinking about it for the rest of the ride. I got out of the car when we reached the hotel, told her goodnight, and went up to the suite. The keys were unnecessary because the front door was open a couple of inches. I held the Walther in my right hand, then pushed the door open just wide enough for me to slip inside. The darkness seemed absolute. I went down onto my knees, with my back against the wall, then fumbled with my left hand above my head until I found the light switch. Nothing happened when the lights came on, so I straightened up again. The living room was empty, so I kept on going into the bedroom.

Tamara was still stretched out on the bed, her face buried in the cushion, and her long blond hair spread like a fan across her bare shoulders.

"What happened?" I asked softly.

She didn't answer. I came up alongside the bed, put my free hand on her shoulder and rolled her over onto her back. Her tongue was a grotesque purple color, held between clenched teeth. Her staring eyes were frantically trying to tell me it wasn't true. I closed my eyes, while my brain gibbered with fury and hatred, and it seemed a hell of a long time before I could force them open again. There was a fine brass wire sunk deep in a fold of flesh around her neck. Whoever had killed her had been some kind of a sadist. They had looped the wire around her neck, taken another small loop—slipped a steel bolt into it—then kept on tightening the bolt until they had strangled her to death.

She had been waiting for the return of her master, I remembered. Her cruel and vicious master, complete with a horsewhip plaited with small steel barbs. Instead, she had gotten a vicious sadistic killer who had slowly strangled her to death. Had it been, I couldn't help wondering, the last and ultimate fantasy of them all?

I went back into the living room. I tripped on the edge of the rug and fell full-length. The glass, full of neat brandy, slipped out of my hand and smashed on the bartop. I neatly sliced two fingers as I swept the pieces away. The pain helped a little, but not very much.

CHAPTER FOUR

"I should never have left her," I said. "I should have told the woman that Karl Madden could wait until morning."

"She's trouble, mate," Hicks said slowly. "She asks you to meet her in that bar and you nearly get killed. Then she asks you to meet Madden, and Tamara gets killed."

"You think Madden hasn't changed sides after all?" I asked.

"Anything's possible, mate." He shrugged expressively, then nodded toward the bedroom. "What are we going to do about her?"

"I don't know," I said truthfully. "We have to be in London by tomorrow night."

"You don't want the police," he said, "and it's too late for them, anyway."

"I laid her out," I said. "Took the wire from around her neck. Dressed her. Closed her eyes. Tried to straighten out her features. She wouldn't have liked to be left looking that way."

"Don't get sentimental on me, mate," Hicks said sharply.

"You're right," I said. "She never mentioned any relatives, or even friends."

"So nobody's going to miss her," Hicks said.

"I won't just dump her body," I told him. "I want it properly disposed of."

"Burial?"

"Or cremation."

His face brightened up a little. "Now you're talking, mate. That's possible."

"How?"

"A nice little touch of arson?" he mused reflectively. "A car accident?"

"Can you guarantee it will burn long enough?" I asked him.

"Do me a favor!" he said impatiently. "What do you think I am? A bleeding amateur?"

"All right," I said. "How do we get her out of the hotel?"

"No problem." He sounded confident. "But I'll need somebody to help me."

"I'll help, naturally!"

"Not you, mate." He shook his head slowly. "Your heart wouldn't be in it, like. Have you got a phone number for Madden?"

"No," I said, then looked at him sharply. "Madden?"

"A bleeding half-million dollars," Hicks said, with great feeling. "It's about time he started earning it!"

"I can give you the address," I said.

He checked his watch. "Sometime late this afternoon," he said, "and I'll need some money. A couple of thousand."

"All right. What are you going to do?"

"I'm not sure yet," he said. "Don't worry. I'll work it out all right. You'd better start getting us organized for London."

"I guess so," I agreed.

"And pack up all her clothes," he said. "Have them ready for when I get back."

Hicks left about fifteen minutes later, complete with his two thousand dollars. I booked us onto a London flight for the following morning, then put a call through to Francine Delato's flat in Knightsbridge. The voice that answered was feminine, and full of aristocratic flattened vowel-sounds. She was a friend of Francine's, she said, and using the flat while Francine was away. She was staying with some friends in Surrey, actually, and, no, she didn't know their names, or the address. What a pity I hadn't rung earlier because Francine had only left late yesterday evening.

I tried to track down Travers and Dryden. It gave me something to do. Mercenaries are rugged individualists, but they do have a couple of clubs—for want of a better word—and they mostly like it to be known where they can be found in case it's a prospective employer inquiring. I drew a blank in Paris, but the guy in Stockholm was a little more helpful. They were relaxing after their last assignment, he believed. They were very close friends, almost inseparable, but perhaps I already knew that? I told him I did. Either London or

Paris, he believed. Perhaps if I tried some of the glossier hotels in each city? It took me another couple of hours to find them, in the London Park Tower. It was Travers I finally got on the other end of the line.

"Paul Donavan," I told him.

"Mr. Donavan?" His voice was strictly neutral.

"I have another assignment for you and Dryden," I told him. "I'll be in London by tomorrow night, and I'll call you then."

"We're having a kind of vacation," he said. "I'm sorry."

"This shouldn't take too long," I said.

"I'm sorry, Mr. Donavan," he said flatly.

"There's something worrying you?"

"Twenty-five out of the thirty, dead," he said. "I knew most of them, Mr. Donavan. None of them were like close friends, but I knew them."

"It's the kind of business you work in," I said. "The kind of business they worked in. You make a lot of money, or you die. They were unlucky."

"Real unlucky, the way I hear it!" A rasp came into his voice. "Rifles that blew up in their faces! Grenades with one-second fuses. Mortars that blew sideways!"

"You figure that was my fault?" I asked softly.

"Mr. Donavan, I'll be honest," he said. "I just don't goddamned well know whose fault it was. But the word's around right now. You're hotter than Hades in the trade. So if it's all the same to you, we'll just continue our vacation."

"Not after I get to London," I told him. "Somebody sabotaged that shipment, Travers. Maybe it was you or your friend, Dryden. Or maybe the both of you."

"You're out of your tiny mind!" he snarled.

"Maybe," I said. "But don't just vanish from your hotel, Travers, because then I'll have to start believing it was you." I hung up on him then, because it seemed the right moment.

I drank some lunch, then packed all of Tamara's things into a couple of suitcases. Then I had a couple of hours sleep in the spare bedroom. It was around five in the afternoon when somebody knocked on the door. I asked who it was, and recognized the voice as he spoke.

"It's Mr. Stoler here, Mr. Donavan." The voice belonged to the hotel manager, and sounded infinitely apologetic. "I'm sorry to disturb you, but the ambulance men are here."

"Ambulance men?" I said blankly.

"Please, Mr. Donavan, you can rely on my absolute discretion," he said. "Doctor Delato was kind enough to call me and explain everything. I completely understand. It's a very unfortunate situation, and it happens all too frequently these days."

"Oh," I said, and opened the door.

I stood to one side as two men in white coats carried a stretcher into the suite and headed toward the bedroom. Stoler came into the room, walking quietly, his thin mustache quivering with sympathy and embarrassment.

"The ambulance is at the back of the hotel," he said. "I told them to take her down in a freight elevator, and I've made sure none of the staff will be around to see them."

"I appreciate that, Mr. Stoler," I said. "You're very kind."

"I wish I could do more, Mr. Donavan," he said earnestly. "Doctor Delato told me how hard you've been trying to help your niece kick the habit. But it's impossible to check on somebody every moment of the day."

"You're right," I said, and sighed deeply.

The two guys in white coats reappeared from the bedroom, carrying Tamara's body on a stretcher. Her head was turned to one side, and a fan of blond hair completely covered her face. Hicks was carrying the front end of the stretcher and Madden the back end. Neither of them looked at me as they went past.

"A tragedy," Stoler said vehemently, after they had gone out into the corridor. "A terrible tragedy, Mr. Donavan!"

"I must get her things," I said. "Doctor Delato said it will be a long stay."

"Allow me," Stoler said quickly. "The very least I can do."

I brought the two suitcases out from the bedroom, and he took them from me.

"Thank you again," I told him.

"I'll see they go with her in the ambulance, Mr. Donavan." His mustache quivered for a moment.

"If there is anything the hotel can do for you, Mr. Donavan, you have only to ask!"

I closed the door on his back, remembering that with Hicks all things were possible, and only very few of them probable. The phone rang around ten minutes later.

"Is Karl with you?" the familiar husky voice asked.

"He was a few minutes back," I said.

"He's been gone for hours already," she said. "What time can I expect him home?"

"Not for a while," I told her. "Sometime tonight."

"I'm bored." Her voice sounded faintly petulant. "It's what they used to call the cocktail hour. Would you like a drink?"

I was going to decline the invitation, then I thought about the bleak hours stretching ahead of me while I waited alone in the hotel suite for Hicks to return.

"Can you make a good martini?" I asked her.

"A seven-to-one mix, chilled; stirred, and not shaken," she said.

"I'll come right over," I told her.

A cab dropped me outside the apartment block on the East River around twenty minutes later. Further down the street, a lamppost was still bent at a crazy angle, like a ludicrous monument to the events of the previous night. I rode the slow elevator up to the penthouse and stopped thinking about Tamara. The wake was over. Nothing I could do would bring her back to life. She died because of her association with me, and I would take revenge for her death. But that would only help me, and not her. When I came to think about it—and it was something I didn't do often—very few of the people I knew lived to enjoy their old age.

Moira Stevens opened the door to me with a tentative smile on her face. Her black hair was still brushed straight back across her head. She was wearing no makeup, and her dark eyes had a bright polished shine to them. The nipple-revealing silk shirt was tucked into the waistband of a miniskirt that showed off her long tapering legs.

"The hell with fashion," she said. "The miniskirt was designed to stay around forever."

"Hello, Mr. Donavan," I said. "Hello, Miss Stevens. Won't you come on in, Mr. Donavan? Thank you, Miss Stevens."

"The social graces? The more banal chitchat that oils the wheels of our lives? And I forgot them! Do forgive me, Mr. Donavan. The martinis await us in the living room, Mr. Donavan. Be so kind as to follow me?"

She turned her back toward me, and I followed her into the living room. The furnishings were unobtrusive, and open French doors led out onto a terrace. She handed me a martini, picked up her own from the bar, then sat down in an armchair. I sat down on the couch facing her and tasted the drink.

"It's very good," I said.

"I met your Mr. Hicks," she said, "but not for long. He spent a quarter of an hour closeted with Karl in the library, then the both of them went out. Karl said he'd be gone for a while, but he didn't say why. I'm curious."

"Stay curious," I told her. "It doesn't concern you."

"You know something?" Her eyes glittered for a moment. "You have to be the rudest bastard I've ever met in my whole life."

"How long have you been with Madden?"

"All my life." She drank some of her drink. "I'm his sister. I had a brief and totally unsuccessful marriage to a guy called Frank Stevens, that lasted all of a couple of months. He was gay and figured marriage would cure him, but it didn't."

"And now you live with Karl?"

"He lives with me when he's not following his profession," she said. "He's the only family I've got and we're very close. Don't misunderstand me about that, either. There's nothing incestuous in our relationship."

"I never presume anything," I said truthfully. "It could get to be a dangerous habit."

"Hicks made me feel nervous just looking at him," she said. "Karl says he's a mercenary, too."

"Ex-mercenary," I said. "Now he's what they used to call a gentleman's gentleman."

"I couldn't figure out who killed the man in the bar," she said. "It was Hicks, wasn't it?"

"Is that why you invited me over for a drink?" I asked her. "To find out for sure?"

"I'm worried about Karl," she said. "I'm sure he's very brave and a very good soldier. But he's not that smart."

"How smart does he have to be?"

"He's not smart enough for what he's gotten himself into with you," she said. "You've got Hicks and all your money to protect you. Karl only has himself."

"He's a professional fighter," I said. "It's the way he earns his living. He's for hire. He just hired himself to me. At very exorbitant rates, I might add."

She bit her lower lip gently. "You could take him off the hook. Pay him something for his information now—nothing like half a million dollars, of course!—and then leave him alone."

"I need him as well as his information," I told her. "I'm sorry."

"Nothing will make you change your mind?"

"Nothing," I agreed.

A soft glow started in the back of her dark eyes. I am not unromantic, but it seemed born out of calculation to me.

"Do you find me attractive?" she asked, in a soft voice.

"Whenever I have the time," I said. "On the previous two occasions I've been in your company, I've been too busy trying to stop from getting myself killed, to notice you much."

"There's nobody in here with a gun." She smiled tentatively. "Nothing to stop your concentration right now."

She got up from the armchair and unbuttoned the silk shirt slowly. When she took it off, she was naked from the waist up. Her breasts were a delicate ivory color; full, and firm, with no sag at all. The coral-colored nipples stood erect, like some kind of a dual challenge.

"I have the strangest feeling that I'm about to make you change your mind," she said.

Then she quickly removed the miniskirt and the brief panties she was wearing underneath. Her body was beautiful. Beneath the proud jutting breasts was a narrow waist that flowered into well-rounded hips. There was a delicious ripe curve to her belly, and a thick bush of curly black pubic hair nestled at the tops of her long tapering legs. She cupped both breasts in her hands, lifting them toward me for a moment, then slowly ran her hands down over her flanks until they cupped her sex.

"Change your mind and you can have all of me," she said. "I won't think of it as any kind of a sacrifice, Paul Donavan. I think I'll enjoy it. You can have me any way you want, and any number of times you want. It's just possible I can do a couple of things you've never even thought of before."

I got up from the couch and put my unfinished drink down on the small table beside it.

"It's a tempting offer," I said, "but no thanks."

"You don't mean it?" Her eyes widened with disbelief.

"Your brother's been attending a funeral," I said, as I headed toward the door. "Ask him whose it was when he gets back."

CHAPTER FIVE

Hicks got back to the hotel suite around eleven that night. He looked a little tired as he made himself a drink, and I didn't bother him with questions. He would tell me in his own time.

"I didn't go out to the house," said. "No point in collecting anything from there if we're going to London."

"Right," I said.

"Bleeding bargain, it was," he went on. "That ambulance, I mean. The bloke who sold it to me couldn't believe his luck."

"Everything went all right?"

"Madden drove the rented car, and I drove the ambulance," Hicks said. "I ran it over a cliff on Long Island. Couple of hundred foot sheer drop to the rocks. We soaked the inside with gasoline before I ran it over. It burned like a torch!" He drank some of his drink. "I waited around to be sure."

"That she was cremated?"

He nodded, then his face reddened slightly. "I

54

said a few words, like. I thought you'd want that."

"A few words?"

"Dust to dust—you know."

"I somehow didn't think you'd know," I said.

"I heard them often enough in the Congo to learn them off by heart. We found the bodies of these nuns at a mission one time"—he grimaced sharply—"but I don't want to remember, now."

"Thank you," I said. "I'm grateful."

"It's the best way. Fire, I mean. Like it's clean. Nothing left to slowly rot and feed the worms and—"

"Yes," I said quickly. "Tell me something. Who the hell was Doctor Delato?"

"Me." He grinned. "Had him eating out of me bleeding hand after a couple of minutes' chat on the phone."

"He believed you were a psychiatrist?" I asked, shaken. "Complete with an East London accent?"

"Delato's a foreign-sounding name, mate," Hicks said, in a smug voice. "So I used a foreign accent to go with it, right?"

"And how is your Italian accent?"

"Italian!" he said scornfully. "I can't even say 'pizza' without making it sound rude. Anyway, all the best nut-doctors are German. Everybody knows that. And I can do a smashing German accent. *Achtung! Schweinhund!* We haf vays of making you talk!"

"That Stoler must be even more naïve than I figured," I said.

The phone rang. Hicks carefully goose-stepped across the room and answered it. "It's that military-looking jerk again," he said, with his hand over the mouthpiece. "Everlasting cock-stand Pace!"

"Tell him to come on up," I said.

Hicks told him, then hung up. "You want me to stay here and listen?" he asked. "Or go into the other room and listen?"

"The other room, I think," I told him. "You worry Pace. He's not sure if you're real."

Pace came marching into the room a couple of minutes later. I made him a drink, with no ice, and he settled himself down on the edge of an armchair.

"There have already been two attempts on your life, I hear," he said. "But both were abortive. My congratulations."

"What brought you the news?" I asked him. "A carrier pigeon?"

He smiled perfunctorily. "We've been keeping an eye on things, of course. But that isn't the reason for my visit."

"My fatal charm?" I wondered out loud. "The free booze?"

"Someone has come up with a new theory," he said. "I thought you should hear it."

"The very least I can do is listen," I told him.

He gave the tip of his nose a sharp tug. "It's very simple, actually. Suppose the shipment was sabotaged after it got ashore? After it left your possession?"

"You said before it would be a peculiar form of mass suicide," I reminded him.

"Not if the saboteur, or saboteurs, took special precautions," he said. "The more obvious one being not to use any of the weapons involved. Or, more likely, to use only the ones you knew you hadn't tampered with."

"Why would somebody do that?"

"There could only be one reason." Pace smiled tolerantly at my lack of understanding. "Somebody had paid them a lot of money to make sure the tribe you were trying to help would lose the war."

"Who would want to do that?"

"Ah!" He tapped the side of his nose roguishly. "That's something we'd dearly like to know, Donavan. I'm hoping you'll be able to help us find out. That is, if the theory is true, of course."

"It would have to be one or more of the survivors," I said.

"Sheppard, DuPlessis, or Madden," Pace said. "Personally, my choice would be DuPlessis. He has more native cunning than the other two put together."

"Then they eliminate me, claiming they're taking their revenge," I said, "and that proves me guilty."

"I thought you'd like it, Donavan," he said, in a faintly patronizing voice. "I don't say it's true, I just say it's viable. You could prove its truth, of course."

"How?"

"By getting the name of their employer," he said. "I'm sure you, and your bully-boy, could persuade him—or them?—to tell the truth? Given the name of their employer, our organization would be only too happy to take care of the rest of it."

"I'll bear it in mind," I told him.

"I felt sure you would." He finished his drink, got up from the armchair, and put the empty glass down on the bartop. "Thank you for the free drink. I'll be pushing along now. You know, it's a funny thing, Donavan, but I get to feeling nervous just being in the same room as you."

"It's a fascinating theory," I said. "I'll certainly see if I can check it out. And you were very welcome to the free drink, Everard."

His mustache twitched sharply the moment before he started toward the door. Hicks came back into the room a few seconds after the door closed in back of Pace.

"I'm hungry," he said. "You want something to eat?"

"A rare steak," I said, "with a green salad on the side."

He called room service and ordered, then made himself a drink. "That Pace," he said. "He's not so bloody stupid as he looks."

"You're right," I agreed. "I'd like to know what he really wants."

"He just told you, mate," Hicks said patiently. "The name of the bastard who hired DuPlessis—

and maybe the other two—to fuck up the shipment."

"But is that what he really wants?" I wondered out loud.

"What the hell else?" Hicks snorted.

It was a good question, and I didn't have any answer. The food arrived around fifteen minutes later, and we ate. Afterward, I lighted a large cigar and had a small Napoleon brandy to keep it company.

"What time is the flight?" Hicks asked.

"Nine-thirty in the morning," I told him. "You'd better order us a car and chauffeur to take us out to Kennedy."

"Right," he said. "I turned in the rented car straight after we got back from Long Island."

"How did Madden perform?"

"He was okay," Hicks allowed, in a grudging voice. "A bit sweaty, like. Especially when we were moving her out of the hotel. Maybe he only feels safe when he's got an armalite rifle in his hands."

"She's his sister," I told him. "She says."

"She's trouble, mate." He helped himself to one of my cigars. "We staying in the usual place in London?"

I nodded. "The Sedan Chair."

"That place makes me curious," he said. "It's always either empty or nearly empty, whenever we stay there. It's tucked into a Kensington side street, and it's bloody expensive, but nobody's ever there. It must lose money hand over bleeding fist!"

"It does," I said. "But it's no more expensive than maintaining a country house, and far more convenient."

"You own it?" His eyes widened a fraction.

"I own it," I said, "but the only people who know I own it are the manager and now you. It also makes a convenient tax loss, and it's a safe place to keep the armory."

"That's something else I wondered about," he said darkly. "How you could produce anything from a hand grenade to a FN auto rifle with a flip of your wrist, like some bleeding magician!"

"We've got one armory in the basement of the Connecticut house, and the other in the cellar of the London hotel," I said. "It beats the hell out of trying to sneak past all those metal detectors."

"You're right," he said.

The phone rang and he answered it. His face was expressionless as he passed it over to me. "Madden," he said. "He sounds like he's upset."

I took the phone and said "Donavan" into the mouthpiece.

"Karl Madden here." His voice was so low-pitched I could only just hear it. "I have to see you right away, Mr. Donavan. It's urgent."

"What about?" I said.

"I can't talk now, not over the phone," he said softly. "Please come over to my apartment right away. Something has just come up and it could make all the difference to what happens in England. I'm not kidding!" Then he hung up.

"I don't bloody well like it," Hicks said, after I'd repeated what Madden had said to him.

"Neither do I, much," I admitted. "But I'll have to go see him."

"We'll have to go," Hicks said.

Riding the slow elevator up to the penthouse, Hicks took his gun out and pulled the trigger once.

"You think so?" I asked.

"Can't be too careful, mate," he said. "What's the matter with you? All this rich living making you soft or something?"

I had the Walther set on double action, so I followed Hicks's example. The elevator came to a stop with a gentle shudder, and I opened the doors. Nobody was waiting to greet us, so we stepped out into the private hallway.

"I'll ring the doorbell," Hicks said. "If this is some kind of a set-up, and somebody's going to open the door with a gun in their hand, it'll confuse them to see me standing here instead of you, right?"

"It might not confuse them enough to stop them pulling the trigger," I said.

"Do me a favor!" he said bitterly.

"Sure," I said, and rang the doorbell.

Hicks swore fervently under his breath, then flattened himself against the wall so he would be invisible to anyone opening the door. I thought about it, then decided if Madden was already feeling nervous, I didn't want to give him a heart attack. So I put the gun back into the belt holster.

The door opened about five seconds later, revealing Moira Stevens, and friend. Moira was wearing nothing but an expression of pure horror on her face, and made small whimpering sounds by way of a greeting. Her friend was standing behind her, one arm wrapped tight around her, giving an unnecessary boost to her full breasts. His other hand held a gun with the barrel pressed hard against the side of her head. Friend was a tall thin character, with a sallow complexion and lackluster pale blue eyes.

"You stupid bastard!" Friend said. "Five more minutes and we'd have left."

"You and Moira?" I inquired.

Behind him, another guy moved into my line of vision, also holding a gun. He was tall and plump, and was sweating a lot. If there's anything I hate, it's somebody nervous holding a gun that's pointing at me.

"So now we're a foursome," I said. "Where's Karl Madden?"

"Come on in," Friend said. "You even look nasty, and this dame gets a bullet through the head."

"I understand," I assured him.

"Close the door!"

I reached out behind me, and pushed. The door closed with a definite clunk. Friend dragged Moira backward, increasing the distance between us. His buddy started to circle around cautiously so he would finish up in back of me. If I had only accepted Hicks's offer in the first place, I reflected, I wouldn't be the pigeon standing around and feeling all naked right now. But it was too late to reverse the roles and he would have to play hero again, and it would leave him more convinced than ever that I was in dire need of a wheelchair and a full-time R.N.

"Play it real cool and both you and the dame get to come out of this alive," Friend said.

"I'm for that," I told him.

The doorbell rang, and just about everybody seemed to stop breathing.

"Who the hell is that?" Friend said finally.

"I wouldn't know," I said. "Are you expecting anybody else?"

"We weren't expecting you, you goddamned stupid—" He took a sudden deep breath. "Answer it!" he said to his buddy.

"Answer it?" The tall fat guy was sweating worse than ever. "What in hell do you mean, answer it?"

"You've got a gun," Friend snarled at him. "Bring whoever it is in here."

"Okay." His buddy swallowed hard, then turned toward the door and reluctantly opened it. "There's nobody here," he said doubtfully, then took another step forward.

Then he just disappeared. One moment he was standing there, and the next moment he was gone.

"Pete?" Friend called hoarsely. "Pete!"

There was no sound from outside the door, and Friend's face began to turn a dirty gray color.

"All right!" he said to me. "Just what the hell is going on?"

"I have no idea," I told him. "You want me to take a look?"

He told me what I could do, and it amounted to just about anything except go take a look.

"You out there!" He raised his voice to a shout. "I've got a gun pressed against this dame's head, and if you don't come in here with your hands in the air by the time I count five, I'm going to pull the trigger. One!" There was no answer. "Two!"

"Hold it!" Hicks's voice called from outside in the corridor. "I'm coming."

The next moment Hicks appeared, propelling the tall fat guy in front of him, one arm wrapped tight around the guy's neck, and his other hand pressing the barrel of his gun hard against the side of the guy's head.

"Small world," Hicks said affably.

"A Mexican stand-off," I said to Friend. "You kill the girl, Hicks kills your buddy, then one of us kills you."

Friend was starting to sweat a little, and not in sympathy with his buddy. "Maybe we can work something out," he said, in a choked voice.

"Like what?" I asked encouragingly.

"Like I let the girl go," he said. "He lets my buddy go, and then the both of us walk out of here."

"It has possibilities," I acknowledged.

©Lorillard 1974

KENT

DELUXE LENGTH
WITH THE FAMOUS MICRONITE FILTER

KENT

PRODUCT OF Lorillard

ng Size or
eluxe 100's.

Micronite filter.
Mild, smooth taste.
America's quality cigarette
Kent.

ngs: 16 mg. "tar," 1.0 mg. nicotine;
0's: 18 mg. "tar," 1.2 mg. nicotine;
enthol: 18 mg. "tar," 1.2 mg. nicotine;
per cigarette, FTC Report Mar '74

Try the crisp, clean taste of Kent Menthol.

The only Menthol with the famous Micronite filter.

"You can't let them go," Moira said, in a high shrill voice. "They killed Karl!"

"You bitch!" Friend moaned. "You goddamned stupid *bitch!*"

He threw her away from him, in a sudden burst of frustrated fury, so she fell flat on her face and went skittering across the tiles. Hicks chose the same moment to throw the tall fat guy straight at the tall thin guy. Friend's automatic reflexes were way ahead of him. He fired two shots and his buddy seemed to stop in midair, hang there for a moment, then fall to the floor.

"It's all your goddamned stupid fault!" Friend screamed at the prone Moira Stevens, then he aimed his gun at her.

There had been just time for me to yank the Walther clear from the belt holster. I aimed for his left shoulder and fired. The trouble was he was still moving, and it was a snap shot. The bullet took him an inch above the left eye, and I guess his future ended right there. Silence prevailed for a full second after his body hit the floor, then Moira Stevens started screaming hysterically and threshing her legs around. Hicks carefully closed the door in back of him, then looked at me.

"It's an old building," he said. "Solid—and soundproofed."

I reached down to help Moira onto her feet and she thanked me by sinking her teeth firmly into my right palm. I managed to prize it loose, then grabbed hold of her ankles and dragged her into the living room. For a change of pace I let go her ankles and sank my fingers deep into her black hair, then pulled her up into a sitting position on the couch. She got her breath back and opened her mouth to start screaming again, so I slapped her hard with my open palm across her bare stomach. It was more confusing than a slap across the face, so she just sat there with her mouth hanging open, staring at me blankly.

"They're both dead," Hicks said, from in back of me.

"Get her a drink," I told him.

"I'll get the three of us a drink, mate," he said.

He came back from the bar a few seconds later with a glass half-full of neat whiskey and gave it to Moira Stevens. She drank a mouthful, shuddered violently, then started to weep softly.

"It's all over," I said. "You don't have to worry anymore."

"Karl," she whimpered, and pointed toward the door leading to the library. "They killed Karl!"

"You take it easy," I said, "and we'll go look."

Karl Madden was sitting in back of the leather-topped desk in the library. His head was slumped forward on his chest, and his gelid blue eyes seemed to be studying the grains of infinity trapped in the leather top. One of our two dead friends had fired at point-blank range into the back of his head. The still-oozing blood was discolored by powder stains.

We went back into the living room, where Moira had stopped crying and was sipping her drink. Hicks picked up his own drink from the bartop, emptied the glass with one practiced swallow, then headed toward the entrance hall.

"I'll be back," he said, over his shoulder.

I picked up my own drink from the bartop and looked at Moira Stevens. "How did it happen?" I asked.

"The doorbell rang," she said, in a small voice. "I was getting undressed in my room, ready to go to bed. Karl called out it was okay, because he was expecting you. The next thing I knew, I heard a shot. I ran out of my room and into the library and there was Karl"—her voice faltered for a moment—"dead, sitting in his chair. And those two men. I hadn't thought about putting any clothes on—I sleep raw, anyway—and they looked at me like I was something they'd just won at the race-track or something! They dragged me back into the living room, threw me onto the floor, and then they were going to rape me, turnabout! But before the fat one could get started, the doorbell rang. You know the rest."

"Who were they?" I asked.

"I don't know." She shook her head slowly. "I've never seen either of them in my whole life before. But Karl must have known them, or he wouldn't have let them in."

"What do you want to do now?" I said.

"Whoever they were, they must have been working for DuPlessis and Sheppard," she said. "They killed my brother. I want revenge, Donavan." She looked up at me, her eyes cold and implacable. "I want to go to London with you and help you find them—and kill them!"

"All right," I said. "You'd better get some clothes on."

"We can't just walk out of here and leave Karl and the others lying dead here!" she exclaimed incredulously.

"My guess is we can," I told her. "We'll figure something out. You were never here. You've been with me since late this afternoon, and you're going to stay the night in my suite. I'll get you a seat on the same morning flight as we're traveling on."

"Okay." She finished her drink, then handed me the empty glass. "I'll go and get dressed. I'll pack a bag, too."

"Do that," I said.

She got up from the couch and walked out of the room. I put her glass back on the bartop and had time to finish my own drink before Hicks came back into the room.

"Catch!" he said, and tossed me a gun.

I caught it. A Smith and Wesson point three-two.

"I'll have the Walther in exchange," he said.

I tossed him the Walther, and put the point three-two into the belt holster. Mine not to reason why.

Hicks held the Walther by the barrel and carefully wiped the butt clean with his pocket handkerchief. "It's not traceable, is it, mate?"

I looked at him.

"Sorry," he said. "Bloody stupid question! The thin one's no problem. He shot his mate with his own gun, right?"

"Right," I said.

"You shot the thin one with the Walther," Hicks continued. "So the Walther becomes the fat one's gun, right?"

"And who shot Madden?" I asked.

"The thin one," he said. "Because the gun you've got now hasn't been fired at all. So—"

"You put the Walther into the fat guy's hand and fire another shot," I said patiently. "So it picks up his prints and puts powder grains into the palm of his hand."

"That's right, Mr. Bleeding Holmes," he growled. "What are you going to do with the bird?"

"She's coming with us," I said. "Back to the hotel and stay the night. And she's been with us since sometime late this afternoon, incidentally. Then she's flying to England with us in the morning."

"You think that's wise, mate?" he asked dubiously. "I've got to fire another shot from the Walther, anyway. Wouldn't it be a bloddy sight easier to put it into her head?"

"Maybe Madden had some genuine information about DuPlessis' plans, and maybe he didn't," I said. "Either way, we'll never know now. But it's possible he confided in his sister."

"You want to get back into the jungle for a while, mate," Hicks said compassionately. "Like I told you before, all this soft living is making a bloody steaming mush out of your brains. You keep on like this, and you'll bust out crying everytime somebody says something nasty."

"Like, piss off?" I asked coldly.

"Or worse." He grinned suddenly. "But it's a pair of tits to be reckoned with, I'll grant you that!"

CHAPTER SIX

New York had been hot and humid. London was warm and humid, with a gentle rain drizzling down. Ten P.M. wasn't a late hour to go visiting, I figured, especially not in Knightsbridge. So I pressed the button beside the name *Delato* and waited.

"Hello?" a tinny voice said through the entry phone.

"I'm Paul Donavan," I said. "A friend of Francine's. I called you yesterday from New York."

"Oh, yes," the voice said. "Come on in."

The buzzer rasped and I pushed the front door open. The flat was on the second floor, and the front door stood open by the time I reached it.

"Do come in, Mr. Donavan," a voice called, from someplace inside. "I'm just putting something on."

I walked into the flat with my mind one big question mark and closed the door in back of me. Francine had refurnished again, I saw, since the last time I had been inside the flat. Now the living room was all Victorian and chintzy, with over-

stuffed armchairs and couch, and a rich-looking
Persian rug on the floor. In the bay window a huge
aspidistra plant stood, looking like it wished it
was a Venus flytrap.

"Sorry to keep you waiting," a voice said, from
in back of me.

I recognized the aristocratic flattened vowel
sounds before I turned around and saw her standing there.

"I'm Angela Hartford," she said. "Francine
kindly loaned me her flat while she's staying with
friends in the country. But I told you that on the
phone, didn't I?"

She was a Viking's dream come true. A tall
girl—around five feet, nine inches, in her bare feet,
I figured—with long flaxen hair that flowed freely
down over her shoulders almost to her waist. Her
eyes were a sparkling china-blue, her cheeks were
fully rounded and glowed with vitality. Her
broad mouth had a slightly overhung lower lip,
and when those lips parted in a smile, flawless
white teeth were revealed. She was wearing thin
silk, something loose that covered her from shoulders to ankles and was overpatterned with a large
floral print against a light beige background. Even
standing still, it was obvious she wore nothing underneath. Her body was a creation of robust perfection. Fat? My mind instantly rejected the
word. Buxom? It would have to do. But everything
was in such magnificent and breathtaking proportion.

"You're the wonderful exciting man who

smuggles guns and starts revolutions and everything," she said. "Francine told me all about you, Mr. Donavan—"

"Paul," I corrected her.

"Paul," she said. "But she left out all the vital details that make all the difference. I mean, for example, she said you were big, but she didn't say none of it is fat. It isn't, is it?"

I took a deep breath and sucked in my waist. "Not one itty-bitty ounce," I lied.

"And I always like men with fair hair," she went on. "Especially big men with fair hair, and that kind of amiable but ruthless look you have. And I never mind a big nose, so long as it's on a big man, either."

"Angela," I said, "I—"

"And those beautiful gray eyes," she said, and sighed deeply. "What fantastic passions lurk in their depths?"

"Angela," I said determinedly, "I—"

"I know!" She pouted ruefully. "You're an American, and you want a drink. Of course! How rude of me. What will you have?"

"Whatever you're having," I muttered.

"I'm not a serious drinker," she confessed. "I hope you don't mind. But I do have a bottle of whiskey—Scotch, I mean!—in the kitchen." Her face brightened again. "And a bottle of Cyprus sherry. I think it's all right because I put some in the soup the other night and it didn't boil or anything."

"A Scotch will be fine," I said. "Over ice?"

"A Scotch on the rocks," she said. "You must keep your idioms right, Paul, or we'll both be confused."

She turned around and swept out of the room—a fantastic sight that jiggled and joggled and bounced and swayed. My mouth dried, just watching her. I walked to the window and looked across at the elegant townhouses the other side of the narrow street for want of something better to do. Something flashed briefly in a window of the house opposite, on the same floor, and I realized I was looking straight at a pair of binoculars the moment before they disappeared.

"Here we are!" a triumphant voice said.

I turned around and saw her put down the tray of drinks onto a small table, its legs hidden by what looked like a curtain of some drab material.

"It's geniune Victorian," the blond said. "Legs were disgusting then, you know? So they invented leg skirts for tables and pianos so nobody had to feel embarrassed. Angela's crazy for Victoriana, as I expect you've noticed. It's all terribly ugly, but then you know what Italians are like. Anything old and ugly always reminds them of their parents, so they just have to buy it and have it around them all the time."

"Did you know there's somebody across the street watching this room with binoculars?" I said.

"Is he at it again?" She walked across to the window and pulled the heavy drapes tight shut.

"I don't mind when I'm here alone, but not when I've got company."

"It doesn't faze you any?" I asked.

"I'm trying to drive him insane," she said complacently. "Some nights I get undressed in front of the window, when I'm sure he's got his binoculars focused. Then, when I'm right down to the buff, I turn around and give him a full frontal and the right gesture to go with it."

"Gesture?" I queried.

"Like this." She swung her hand toward me with the first two fingers fully extended. "Does it mean the same in American?"

"I'm not sure," I said. "What does it mean in English?"

"Get fucked," she said nonchalantly. "But not by me, of course. Then I pull the drapes tight shut and leave him foaming at the mouth with frustration. Francine thought it might be a good idea to invite him over one night, then drop the aspidistra on his head while he was ringing the entry phone. But I think my way is more subtle. You know, more Machiavellian, don't you think?"

"I don't give a goddamn if you're right or wrong," I said sincerely. "I think you have to be the most gorgeous girl I've ever met."

"Thank you, Paul." Her eyes sparkled even more brightly. "Isn't this too, fantastic? Francine bought it last week and they only delivered it yesterday. Now I'll have the chance of finding out if it's as good as everybody says it is."

"Just what, exactly, are we talking about?" I ventured.

"The water bed," she said. "I slept on it last night, of course, but that's not the same thing, is it? I mean it's just not what a water bed is designed for."

The one small ice cube in my drink had already disappeared, I noticed, as I raised the glass to my lips. So now the Scotch only tasted lukewarm, as opposed to warm, and I supposed it was an improvement.

"I'm jumping my fences too quickly, aren't I?" Angela said, her voice full of self-reproach. "I mean, we should get through the conversation first and then make our way toward the water bed. What did you want to see me about?"

"I guess I had a reason," I said. "It doesn't seem to be important now."

"Something about Francine?" she wondered. "I hate to remind you of that Italian doll at a moment like this, but after all she is my friend, and if it hadn't been for her I wouldn't have met you, would I?"

"You know where she's staying?" I asked.

"With friends in Surrey," she said. "I'm sorry, that's all I do know. She's always vague about details. She did say she'll be back around the end of next week."

"I guess I'll find her," I said vaguely.

"Where are you staying?" she asked.

"A hotel in Kensington," I said.

"Will anybody be worried if you don't go back tonight?"

"Maybe I should make a call," I said.

"Of course." She nodded slowly. "I don't mean to pry into your private life or anything, Paul, but does that mean you have another girl staying at the hotel?"

"No," I said. "There's a man who could be worried if I don't show, and he doesn't hear from me."

"Oh?" She bit hard down on her lower lip, then slowly brightened again. "Well, all that wonderful stuff Francine told me about the way you perform couldn't be all lies, could it? For all I know, a bisexual is just a little more sophisticated, perhaps?"

"It's nothing like that!" I snarled at her.

"I'm glad," she said. "I know I'm old-fashioned and everything, but I was at a party once and a lesbian sneaked her hand up my skirt when I wasn't looking."

"What did you do?" I asked curiously.

"I just closed my thighs and held her hand there," Angela said, in a tranquil voice. "Then I kept on asking in a loud voice what she thought she was doing. There must have been about fifty other people in the same room, and by the time I let go of her hand, they were all waiting to hear her answer, too."

"What happened then?"

"She ran out of the room, crying," she said. "I thought it would teach her a lesson to be more careful the next time. I mean, I always make sure a man isn't queer before I let him know I'm interested, because it's an insult to him otherwise."

"And I always figured my education was complete," I said, in a wondering voice.

"You make your phone call, and I'll make sure the water bed is ready for action," she said briskly. "The bedroom's the second door on the left when you've finished, and if you're in any doubt, just listen for the water music."

She turned around and swept out of the room. Again, I watched that fantastic sight of a shimmering floral print jiggling and joggling and bouncing and swaying, until she vanished out of sight. I picked up the phone, dialed the hotel's number, then spoke with Hicks.

"There's some that has all the bleeding luck, and there's some who wouldn't be able to get a hard-on if it was raining crumpet," he said sagely, when I told him I wouldn't be back until sometime in the morning.

"You ever sleep on a water bed?" I asked casually.

"Not bloody likely!" he said. "And you want to be careful, mate."

"How do you mean?"

"Just don't go getting excited," he said warningly. "You'll do yourself a nasty injury if you're not careful."

"I'll be careful," I promised. "How is Moira Stevens?"

"Exhausted, she said, and gone to bed. I'm organized, mate. If she tries to leave the hotel or make any phone calls, I'll know about it."

"Fine," I said, and hung up.

I hesitated when I reached the second door on the left and figured maybe it was politic to knock, so I knocked. Angela's voice said for me to enter, so I did. The water bed seemed to dominate the whole room. It was massive—around five by eight feet—and covered with a black silk sheet. A heap of cushions at the far end were covered with the same material.

"It's the contrast between the white bodies and the black silk," Angela said evenly. "I don't know how you feel about it, but Francine swears it's guaranteed to drive any redblooded Italian clean out of his mind. But then I think all Italian men are a little naïve. They start pinching bottoms before puberty, and it stunts their imaginations."

She was sitting in front of the dresser mirror, idly brushing her hair. The floral print made a soft heap on the rug at her feet. Light from the table lamp cast a warm glow across the alabaster whiteness of her back. I suddenly felt over-dressed. It didn't take long to rectify the situation. Angela put down her brush, stood up, then turned toward me.

"You're the living proof of the cliché, did you know?" she asked.

"Which one is that?"

"The one about men with big noses always have big ding-dongs to match," she said.

She moved closer toward me, then reached out

with one hand and grasped me firmly. It was all that was needed to complete the erection.

"Ding-dong?" I said. "What the hell kind of a description is that?"

"Very apt," she said. "You ding with your ding-dong, and dong when your ding-dong dings."

"I had to ask!" I muttered.

She put her arms around my neck and her lips pressed hard against mine. I could feel the soft but firm weight of her breasts squashed up against my chest, and slid my hands down over her flanks and cupped the generously rounded cheeks of her bottom firmly. I walked her slowly backward toward the bed until we fell onto it and bounced gently. Her body was an absolute delight; her large nipples firmed under my tongue, while she made soft murmurings of appreciation. Our lovemaking progressed, while the water bed undulated and gurgled its benign appreciation. Everybody was appreciating. Then later, she released my head from the scissorlike grip of her legs and rolled me over onto my back. The next moment she lay on top of me, deftly slid my shaft into the moist secret haven between her legs, and smiled down at me.

"Why don't we see if we can make waves?" she said.

The tumultuous climax left us bobbing up and down, and temporarily exhausted. We lay there side by side for what seemed a long time, then Angela raised herself into a sitting position.

"I shall return, with refreshments," she said solemnly, "and something special for round two."

She came back into the room a few minutes later, carrying a tray. There was a bottle of vintage Bollinger and two champagne glasses. Also a plate of hot buttered toast, cut into delicate fingers, and heaped with black caviar. There was also an outsize aerosol can of men's shaving foam. I sincerely hoped we weren't about to eat it.

By the time we had demolished the toast and about half the bottle of champagne, I was beginning to feel randy again. By the way Angela's fingers were busy conducting an intimate exploration, she felt the same way. She put the tray onto the top of the bureau, ripped off the black silk cover and cushions from the water bed, then picked up the aerosol can of foam.

"Don't you dare shave it off," I told her, and I looked at the delicate fuzz of honey-colored hair between her legs. "I like it just the way it is."

"There's this Chinese girlfriend of mine," she said happily. "She says it's absolutely fantastic, and not horribly messy at all like oil."

"Is that right?" I said.

"She says if you think you've done everything, try this with a water bed," Angela went on, still talking some language I didn't understand.

I opened my mouth to say something, then changed my mind and closed it again. Angela carefully sprayed the whole surface of the bed until it was covered with white foam, then sprayed the front of herself from shoulders to knees. While I was still watching her with my mouth sagging open, she did the same thing to me.

Her Chinese girlfriend was dead right, I discovered a couple of minutes later. Sliding around in all that foam added a kind of unique dimension to lovemaking. When you thought you had a firm grip on something tender, you didn't. The ultimate union became strictly impermanent. It was exciting. The both of us slipping and sliding all over the bed, and looking like Daddy and Mummy Christmas gone berserk. It got to the point where I couldn't stand it any longer.

"Ghengis Khan!" I said. "That's me. Murderer and pillager, robber and raper! I now claim my victim!"

I slid off the bed, then arranged Angela precisely in the center of it with her arms outstretched, and her legs wide apart.

"I'm sure this is going to be bags of fun," she said doubtfully, "but what, exactly, are you going to do, Ghengis?"

"Just watch, and you'll find out," I told her.

I backed away from the bed toward the door. There still wasn't quite enough of an approach, I figured, so I opened the door wide and backed out into the hallway.

"Paul?" Angela sounded a little nervous for some reason. "What are you going to do now?"

"Don't worry about a thing," I said happily. "This is going to be a totally new experience for you in the area of ultimate exotic pleasure."

I took a deep breath, yelled, *"Geronimo!"* and charged. My shaft waved firecely in the breeze, scattering small blobs of white foam ever-which-way as I went. Angela's eyes dilated with horror as she saw me hurtling toward the water bed, but I just didn't care.

"Geronimo!" I yelled again, and launched myself into a lunging dive across the foot of the water bed.

"Oh, no!" Angela yelled, in stark terror. "Not that!"

The next moment she rolled herself over in a frantic and convulsive effort, so she fell off the edge of the bed. I hit the foam-covered surface of the bed face-down and spread-eagled, and just kept right on going along the whole goddamned length of the stupid thing. There was no friction to slow me down—absolutely nothing to stop my speedy progress from one end to the other. But everything has to come to a stop, I realized a split-second later as the solid wall at the far end of the bed loomed rapidly into sight. The front of my head slammed into it with appalling force, and there was a moment of horrendous pain before the world blacked out around me.

CHAPTER SEVEN

Hicks looked at the large dark bruise in the center of my forehead and shook his head slowly.

"You got excited again, mate," he said.

"Maybe just a little," I said grudgingly. "It was the imperfect end to a perfect night."

"Did you see a doctor?" he asked.

"What the hell would I have told a doctor?" I asked savagely. "She chickened out at the last moment, so there was nothing to stop me skidding the whole length of this foam-covered water bed and smashing my head against the wall at the far end."

"Bloody hell!" he said compassionately. "Somebody should give you a Purple Heart for that, mate!"

Finchley, the hotel manager, materialized out of nowhere, as usual. He is a small man with glossy black hair, a thin mustache, and a sallow pitted complexion. Before he came to work for me, he managed one of the largest gaming houses in London. Security is his middle name.

"If I might have a word, Mr. Donavan?" he asked softly.

"Of course," I told him.

"There is a message for you," he said. "I'm very sorry I didn't deliver it when you arrived last night. Unfortunately, you were in and out of the hotel so quickly—"

"Never mind," I said.

"It's been here for some time—three weeks or more. The instructions were to deliver the message to you personally when you arrived at the hotel."

"Okay," I said patiently. "What message?"

"From a Mr. Nkrudu," he said, "of the Malagaian Embassy. He wishes you to contact him," Finchley said, with great formality. "His secretary gave me to understand that although it would obviously have to await your arrival in this country, it was of the greatest importance you contact him as soon as possible once you were here."

"That's all?" I asked.

"That's all," he agreed.

"You have any idea where his embassy is situated?"

"Victoria Grove," he said. "Just four streets from here, Mr. Donavan."

"Thanks," I said. "How is Miss Stevens?"

"Very comfortable, I think." He stroked his thin mustache carefully. "She remained in her room all night and made no telephone calls. Breakfast was served to her in her room an hour ago."

"Fine," I said.

He retreated back into his office, leaving Hicks and myself alone in the small hotel lobby.

"That's very interesting, mate," Hicks said. "Like, if an embassy is territory belonging to the country that owns it, can they string you up from the chandelier and get away with it?"

"I hope not," I said truthfully. "Maybe I should go see him right now and find out."

"I'll come with you," Hicks said promptly.

"I don't figure there's any real danger," I said. "If the Malagaians were after my blood, they wouldn't issue a formal invitation to go see their ambassador at their embassy."

"Maybe they've imported a witch doctor to put the green mockers on you," Hicks said brightly.

"I'll walk around there now and find out," I said. "It shouldn't take long."

"All right," Hicks said reluctantly. "Did you find out anything last night?"

"She doesn't know anymore than she told me over the phone," I said. "Francine is staying with friends someplace in Surrey."

"It's about time we had a little heart-to-heart with that Stevens crumpet," he said. "I could do that while you're gone."

"Better wait until I get back," I said. "I think we should try the gentle approach first."

"I could have her all docile and licking your feet by the time you get back with no trouble at all!"

"Let it wait," I said.

"All right," he said, "but there are times when

you make me feel really pissed-off. You know that?"

It took around ten minutes to walk to Victoria Grove. The sun was shining, a gentle breeze was blowing, and my forehead throbbed with every step. The embassy was open for business. I gave my name to a lady in a flowering kaftan, who wore thin gold-rimmed glasses and had the deep suspicious stare of every professional secretary. Within two minutes, she ushered me into Mr. Nkrudu's office.

He was a tall handsome man, his skin so black it looked a deep blue. The tribal scar on his left cheek didn't quite match the faultless perfection of his Saville Row suit, and his deep baritone voice was accentless. A graduate of Oxford or Harvard, I figured, and probably an honors graduate at that.

"Mr. Donavan." He shook my hand vigorously. "It's an honor to meet you, sir. Won't you please sit down?"

I sat down in a comfortable armchair, facing him across his desktop. He smiled delightedly at me, flashing brilliant white teeth, and shook his head a couple of times in obvious delight. I began to get the uneasy suspicion I must be the wrong Mr. Donavan.

"I arrived in London last night," I said. "Your message said to contact you—"

"As soon as possible," he said. "I'm delighted you did, sir. Delighted!"

"Are you sure I'm the right Mr. Donavan?"

"Mr. Donavan"—he placed his elbows on the desktop and steepled his fingertips—"let me be frank with you. There was a time when we did not consider you to be a friend of our country. I must ask you to forgive us for that dreadful mistake. As you know, since we have achieved independence, our country has unfortunately been plagued with internal dissension."

"A tribal situation," I said. "The Nkria were in the majority and occupied the hinterland. The Imroda were in the minority and occupied the rich and fertile seacoast."

"And the Nkria being, as you say, the majority, formed the government," he said. "A democratic process, Mr. Donavan."

"After they had murdered most of the Imroda leaders, who happened to be the intellectuals of the country and perhaps were naïve enough to believe in a democratic form of government."

"A specious argument, Mr. Donavan." He shook his head slowly, with a look of deep regret on his face. "Although they talked of democracy with their tongues, in their hearts they wished to keep their rich possessions on the coast, and not share their wealth with their poorer brothers of the interior."

"Well," I allowed, "you sure took care of that."

"You are sparring with me, Mr. Donavan." He smiled benignly. "Your words do not echo the feelings of your heart. Please allow me to come to the point. You know that recently there was an armed insurrection in my country. The Imroda were backed by a small band of white mercenaries and a large shipment of arms. The rebellion was put down, I'm happy to say."

"And followed by a bloody massacre," I said.

"I assure you it's not so," he said. "We hung their leaders, naturally. If you don't hang their leaders, they think you haven't taken them seriously and it excites them to further folly. There were, I grant you, the isolated excesses. Regrettably, a few women were raped, and probably the odd child was put to the bayonet. But no really vindictive punishments were enacted. The rebellion was put down very quickly, and we were very pleased about that. So there was no *need* for savage retaliation. Within a week of the last bullet being fired, everything was back to normal. But things could have been very different!"

"How?" I asked him.

"You're sparring with me again, Mr. Donavan." He made a small self-deprecating gesture with both hands. "So be it, if you wish. Had the shipment of arms not been sabotaged, then things could have been very different, indeed. Under the leadership of the mercenaries, and backed by a very significant fire power, the Imroda could have devastated half the country before they were overcome. But the fact that the arms had been tampered with to the point where they were dangerous to the users made all the difference. It destroyed the morale of the mercenaries and so doubly destroyed the morale of the Imroda. Given that situation, our victory was assured, almost before the first shot was fired."

"So?" I asked.

"So we are thankful to the man who sabotaged the shipment," he said. "A man who must be a true Malagaian patriot, at heart. We wish to show our thanks in a practical manner. We are, as you well know, a small and impoverished country. So we can only make a small gesture, in no way commensurate with the effort our patriot himself has made. But we sincerely hope he will receive the miserable token of our thanks in the manner in which it is given."

He opened a desk drawer, took out a sealed envelope, and gave it to me.

"What's this?" I asked blankly.

"The number of the Swiss bank account," he said, "where we have deposited one hundred and fifty thousand American dollars to your credit."

"To my credit?" I mumbled.

"Of course," Nkrudu said patiently. "You are the patriot who sabotaged the shipment of arms."

"What the hell makes you think that?" I said, in a choking voice.

He smiled tolerantly. "We know," he said. "Beyond any shadow of a doubt, we know. And how we know is not important, Mr. Donavan."

I forced myself to take a long hard look at his face. He wasn't putting me on. He meant every goddamned word he'd just said. There would be no point in denying it, I realized, and no point in making useless gestures.

"Thank you," I told him, and put the envelope into the inside pocket of my coat.

"We only wish we could do more to thank you for your magnificent help, Mr. Donavan," he said. "You may rest assured that if you wish to visit our country at any time, you will be given a most splendid welcome."

"Thanks again," I said. "I'm curious about one thing—your source of information."

"Was impeccable," he said. "I can tell you no more than that, I'm afraid."

We parted with a firm handshake, and for a moment there, I almost felt guilty about not sporting a tribal scar as did my brother compatriot. I walked back slowly through the hot sunshine to the hotel, feeling like some kind of Judas. Only a few women had been raped, and only the odd child put to the bayonet? And there was Paul Donavan being thanked for his help and given one hundred and fifty thousand dollars for his trouble.

Hicks was waiting for me in the bar off the hotel lobby, drinking a pint of warm English beer. I told the bartender I would have a vodka and pure apple juice, with ice, in a tankard, and being a good bartender, he didn't even twitch.

"How was the witch doctor?" Hicks asked.

"Don't ask," I said. "I don't want to even think about it."

"Bad, eh?"

"Worse than you can ever imagine," I said. "Malagai thanks me for sabotaging the shipment. They are so delighted with me, they've put a lot of money into a Swiss account for me, as a token of their thanks."

Hicks almost choked on a mouthful of beer and sprayed white foam across the table. It somehow reminded me of the previous night and my forehead started to throb again.

"What the bloody hell makes them think you did it?" he asked.

"I tried real hard to find out," I said. "Nkrudu got all coy about it. His source of information was impeccable, he said."

"DuPlessis?"

"Maybe." I shrugged helplessly. "I'd give a lot to know just who, exactly."

"So what do we do now?" Hicks demanded.

"Try and find out where Francine is and keep her out of trouble," I said. "We should talk with Moira Stevens."

"She'll be down to join us for a drink in a minute," he said. "She was going to join me for an intimate drink, but you had to get back too bloody early!"

The brunette came into the bar a few minutes later. Her hair was brushed straight back across her head, her dark eyes had that bright polished look about them again, and she looked fresh and sparkling with no makeup. She was wearing a bronze-colored shirt, and black bell-bottom pants. Thin copper hoops clung to her earlobes and the whole outfit gave her a strong resemblance to some kind of a female buccaneer. She sat down at the table, told the hovering bartender she would have a dry martini, then looked at me.

"Has somebody been trying to kill you again?" she asked, in a mild voice.

"With ecstasy," Hicks said, and choked on his beer.

"It was an accident," I said tersely. "How are you feeling?"

"Rested," she said. "What are we going to do, now we're in England?"

"How much did your brother tell you?" I asked her. "About DuPlessis and Sheppard and their future plans?"

The bartender served her drink, and she waited until he was back behind the bar before she spoke.

"They intend kidnapping the girl—what's her name?"

"Francine Delato," I said.

She nodded. "Her. Then they'll use her as bait to attract the both of you, so they can kill you."

"Your brother told me that much," I said. "How? When? Where?"

"What's the date today?" she asked.

"August 29," I told her.

She grimaced. "It's tomorrow, then."

"Where?"

"A place in the country," she said.

"In Surrey." I drank some of my drink to stop myself from getting irritated. "Where, in Surrey?"

"It had a funny name." She thought for a few

seconds. "Little Charming? No. Little Chalmouth, that's it."

"What are the names of the friends she's staying with in Little Chalmouth?" I asked.

"I don't know." She bit down on her lower lip gently. "Karl never told me the complete details. I guess he figured there was no particular reason why he should."

"Did he say how they were going to kidnap her?"

"They found out she likes to ride horses, and her friends have a stable. So they figured on kidnapping her when she was out riding, and alone."

"What are they going to do with her afterward?"

"Keep her at a lonely farmhouse someplace. Karl said they had already located one and were renting it."

"Where?"

She shrugged helplessly. "I don't know."

"Christ!" Hicks said. "You're a bloody great help, you are."

"I'm sorry," she said coldly. "But it's like I said—Karl never told me all the details because he didn't think it would be necessary for me to know."

Finchley glided into the bar with an apologetic look on his face. "I'm sorry to disturb you, Mr. Donavan. There's a young lady on the telephone, asking for you. She said you know her." His eyebrows lifted a fraction. "She said to tell you she is the Florence Nightingale of the water-bed set."

I ignored the sudden spluttering wheeze from Hicks and followed Finchley out into the lobby.

"Paul, darling," Angela's voice purred into the phone when I answered it. "How is your poor head today?"

"Throbbing," I said, "but I figure I'll live."

"Such a tragic waste," she said, "and it was all my fault, really. But right at the last moment I got this sudden picture of myself pinned to the wall forever, like a butterfly in some hideous little man's private collection. It's such a *big* ding-dong you have, darling!" She laughed, a low gurgling sound. "Have you seen Francine?"

"No," I said. "Have you?"

"No," she said, "but she's back. She must be. Her friends rang a few minutes ago for her. The ones she's been staying with down in Surrey. They seemed surprised she wasn't at the flat."

"When did she leave?"

"Early last night, rather suddenly I gather, before dinner. They sounded quite put out. Francine didn't bother saying good-bye, apparently. She just upped and left. They wanted to know if she was going to send for her clothes and things."

"Did they get the horse back?" I asked dully.

"Horse, darling? What horse?"

"Never mind," I said. "It was just a thought."

"Well—I know I'm crazy to even offer!—but if she does turn up at the flat, shall I get her to give you a ring?"

"Please," I said. "And thanks for calling, Angela."

"Just hurry up and get your poor head better," she said. "I think we can work it out, you know? If we pile all the cushions up against the wall, and you don't take such a long run, then I—"

I hung up gently while she was still talking, and walked back into the bar. The both of them waited patiently while I sat down and finished my drink.

"I guess they moved it up a couple of days," I said finally.

"They've got her?" Hicks said.

I repeated the essential elements of the conversation with Angela.

"They've got her, all right," Hicks said. "So what the bloody hell do we do now?"

"You go round to the Park Tower Hotel and see Travers and Dryden," I said. "Tell them what's happened, and tell them I want their services as of now."

"All right," Hicks said, "and if they're not with you, they're bleeding well against you, right?"

"Right," I said.

He got up from the table and started walking toward the lobby. Moira Stevens watched him go, then lighted a cigarette.

"What will you do now?" she asked.

"Sit around and wait for them to contact me," I said. "What the hell else can I do now?"

"It's all too late," she said. "Is that what you mean?"

"I guess I do," I said.

"At least it's better than New York," she said. "Here, people aren't trying to kill you all the time."

"Not yet," I said.

CHAPTER EIGHT

"Scarpered!" Hicks said disgustedly. "Done a bunk! Cleared out. No forwarding address, no bleeding nothing!"

"They're nervous," I said. "Don't want to get involved."

"More than that," Hicks said darkly. "They've been got at, mate. Warned off! So what do we do now?"

"Have a late lunch," I said.

"Where's the crumpet?" He looked around the bar as if he expected to see Moira Stevens hidden inside the nearest tankard.

"Gone out for a walk," I said.

"You let her go?" He looked at me disbelievingly.

"Why not?" I said. "She's not important any-more. Her information wasn't only useless, it was also outdated."

"I suppose you're right," he said reluctantly. "So what are we going to do after the late lunch?"

"Wait," I said. "DuPlessis has to contact me sometime. He must know I'm here. He seems to know everything else. Have you thought about that?"

"What?" Hicks growled.

"He knows a hell of a lot more about Francine than I know about Francine," I said. "He knows her friends in the country. He knows she's going to stay with them, and from when to when, for how long. He knows they have a stable and she likes to ride a horse. He even knows she likes to go riding by herself."

"You're trying to tell me something, mate?"

"I'm just wondering how the hell it is that everybody else is better informed than I am," I said. "And I do include Mr. Nkrudu in that, too."

We ate the late lunch, and neither of us seemed to be in good appetite. The afternoon dragged on, with both of us sitting in the living room of my suite. I gave up trying to read a newspaper when I realized I had read the same paragraph four times over. Hicks was totally involved with a glove puppet show on television, and I envied him. Sometime late in the afternoon the phone rang, and I answered it on the second ring.

"Mr. Donavan," a bass voice said. "My name is DuPlessis. Alexei DuPlessis. I have a friend of yours with me, and she wants to talk with you."

There was a few seconds silence, then I heard the familiar enchanting liquid tones of Francine's voice in my ear.

"Hello, Paul." She sounded slightly breathless. "I just wanted to let you know I'm all right."

"They kidnapped you?"

"Yes," she said. "But they haven't hurt me at all. They've really been very nice to me."

"Where are you?"

"I don't know. After they kidnapped me they put this horrible needle into my arm and I didn't wake up again until I was here." She laughed softly. "Wherever here is."

"Try not to worry," I said weakly. "I'm sure we'll be able to work something out."

"*Caro mio*," she said softly, "I do hope so. They keep on telling me of all the unspeakable things they will do to me if you don't cooperate with them."

"They? How many of them are there?"

There was a muffled grunt, a scuffling sound, and then DuPlessis came back on the line.

"Don't try and get cute, Donavan," he said. "You wouldn't want her to get hurt, right?"

"What do you want?" I asked him.

"To talk first," he said. "I meet you someplace, the girl stays here with somebody looking after her. If I don't get back, my friend cuts her throat. It's real simple."

"Where do we talk?"

"Your hotel," he said; "tonight. Around nine. I'll bring a friend."

"All right," I said. "Here, at nine."

"If you're getting any smart ideas, forget them," he said harshly. "I don't need you, Donavan, you need me. Remember that. If I have to, I'll kill you, and have the girl as some kind of consolation prize afterward."

I looked at Hicks after I had put the phone down, and he shook his head admiringly.

"I just don't know how he does it, honest!" he said. "Five different voices and I didn't even see his bleeding lips move!"

"That was DuPlessis," I said, and tried not to snarl. Then I repeated the essence of the conversation.

"He wants something else," Hicks said, after I had finished, with deep conviction in his voice. "Not just revenge."

"Like what?" I said.

"I dunno. He's psycho, mate. You want to watch that."

"We want to watch him after he leaves the hotel," I said.

"No chance." Hicks shook his head decisively. "If he's using a car, he'll leave it in the West End someplace and come the rest of the way by public transport—bus or tube. And when he leaves, his friend will probably hang about to make sure DuPlessis isn't followed."

"So we follow his friend," I said.

"And finish up in another hotel for the night?" Hicks rolled his eyes. "Do me a favor, mate! I know this bastard."

"Suppose we take the both of them and torture the truth out of one of them?" I asked.

"He'll've thought of that," Hicks said. "Maybe he'll have a couple more blokes outside the hotel. If he's not out inside the hour, they come in. Anyway, it wouldn't work. You could spend the rest of your bleeding life checking out all the lying stories he told you about where the girl is, right?"

"Is he vulnerable in any area? Family, wife, anything like that?"

"Not on your nellie!" Hicks sneered. "There's only three things DuPlessis is interested in; screwing people, hurting people, and killing people."

"He's a sadist," I said. "He doesn't want to kill us in a hurry, right? So maybe the meeting tonight is only the beginning."

"Maybe." Hicks shrugged. "One thing's for sure, mate. He won't ever give you the girl back, not alive, anyway."

"Francine is a nice girl," I said. "I wouldn't want anything to happen to her."

"You still don't understand," he said soberly. "Having DuPlessis after your blood is like being chased by a mad dog, mate. The only way you're going to stop the bastard from killing you is by killing him first."

"I don't want Francine hurt," I said obstinately.

"Now I know why somebody called you Sir Lancelot." He rolled his eyes slowly. "At the time I was stupid enough to think they were talking about the way you can't stop chasing women!"

"That's your only advice?" I asked coldly. "Kill DuPlessis, and never mind about what happens to Francine?"

"That's right, mate," he said softly, then turned his attention back to the television.

They arrived promptly at nine that night. Finchley had been primed to hold their attention at the front desk long enough for Hicks to sneak out of Finchley's office, from behind them, put a gun to their backs, and frisk them. Meantime, I was waiting up in the suite with a drink in my hand. An employer still has some rights.

The door opened and they came into the room with Hicks in back of them. He closed the door, then leaned against it.

"They're clean," he said.

The one who had to be DuPlessis was almost bald and sported heavy bright ginger-colored muttonchop whiskers as some kind of compensation. His skin was leathery, a deep brown color, and his eyes were a dull opaque gray. He was big—running to fat—but there was still a hell of a lot of muscle left.

"I am Alexei DuPlessis," he said, in a thick voice. "And you must be Donavan, of course."

"Of course," I agreed with him.

"And this is my friend," he added. "Hank Sheppard."

Sheppard was tall and lanky, somewhere in his early thirties, and emanated a boyish kind of enthusiasm. He had a deceptively open-looking face and wide innocent blue eyes. There's always a Hank Sheppard at the forefront of a crowd that's just witnessed a fatal road accident. He's the one who's still licking his lips.

"So who's minding the store?" I asked.

DuPlessis grinned broadly. His teeth were very large and mostly yellow. "No need," he said. "We left her tied to the bed with a gag in her mouth, and naked. But it's a warm night, so far. She has a very beautiful body, Donavan. You must have been sorry when that long voyage was finished."

"So there's just the two of you," I said gently.

"We're the principals," he said, "but we have hired some other help. They're hanging around outside the hotel right now, just in case you were thinking of doing something stupid." He gestured toward the bar. "Get us a drink, Hank. I wouldn't trust his goddamned butler not to spill them on the rug!"

Sheppard moved across to the bar. DuPlessis settled himself comfortably on the couch, then took his time about lighting a large cigar. His friend brought the drinks back, gave one to Du-Plessis, then sat down beside him on the couch.

"You've got Francine Delato," I said. "I don't want her hurt. The next move is up to you."

In back of DuPlessis, I saw Hicks roll his eyes upward toward the ceiling while his lips moved silently.

"You should have been there, Donavan," Du-Plessis said. "Malagai, I mean."

"Everybody keeps on telling me that," I said.

"They'd pull the trigger and the gun would explode in their hands and kill them," he said. "Some of the grenades exploded a second after the pin was pulled, before the guy holding it had a chance to throw it. A lot of guys were killed like that, Donavan. Thirty white mercenaries, and only five survived. You owe us for that, Donavan. You owe us a hell of a lot!"

"Donavan didn't do it, mate," Hicks said sharply. "It must have been done after the shipment was landed. My bet is it wasn't done by anybody who got killed!"

"It's amazing," Sheppard said brightly. "A real live speaking dummy. You figure Donavan is a ventriloquist, Alexei? If he is, he's goddamned good! I didn't even see his lips move."

"I was going to kill you, Donavan," DuPlessis said, "but I changed my mind. Now I want compensation. So does Hank. Isn't that right, Hank?"

"Money." Sheppard smiled shyly. "I want a lot of money, Donavan. Enough so I never have to risk dying in some disease-ridden hole like Malagai ever again."

"How much?" I asked.

"We figured it out," DuPlessis said. "Two hundred thousand dollars each, and our expenses. It took us a lot of time and trouble to set this thing up. Say, an even half-million?"

"In cash," Sheppard said. "We don't care about the currency too much. Either American dollars or British pounds will do."

"For that you get the girl back," DuPlessis said, "and—for a big bonus—you get to keep on living."

"It would take me a little while to raise that kind of money." I said.

"The day after tomorrow," DuPlessis said comfortably. "A rich tycoon like you, Donavan? That's more than enough time."

"All right," I said.

"There's this cute little villlage called Little

Chalmouth," he said. "There's a hotel—what do they call them in this goddamned country?"

"A pub," Hicks said tonelessly.

"His lips didn't move that time either," Sheppard said, in an admiring voice.

"Pub, called the Blue Boar," DuPlessis continued. "We'll meet you there at noon the day after tomorrow. You bring the money, we'll take you to the girl."

"I need some kind of a guarantee," I said mildly. "That after I've given you the money, I'll be able to leave with the girl, both of us still alive."

"Nothing can happen in the pub," DuPlessis said easily. "Not with all those other people around. Show me the money, then leave it with your dummy, Hicks, in the bar, and Hank can keep him company. That way, nobody gets to be cute while we're gone. You and me go get the girl, then the three of us come back to the pub. You tell your dummy everything is okay, we collect the money, and you bring the girl back to London."

"All right," I said. "The Blue Boar in Little Chalmouth at noon, the day after tomorrow."

There was a discreet knock on the door and everybody froze momentarily. Hicks moved to one side quickly, his gun held ready, then jerked the door open. Moira Stevens walked into the room, then came to a sudden stop as she saw the company.

"I'm sorry," she said. "Am I interrupting something?"

"We were just about finished," I told her.

"I'll say one thing for you, Donavan," DuPlessis said. "You sure have good taste in women!"

He got up from the couch, and Sheppard got up with him. If it's possible for two people to surround somebody, they did just that to the brunette.

"Like a rattlesnake in bed, I bet!" DuPlessis said.

"Big tits, like the Italian piece!" Sheppard said, with boyish enthusiasm. "I wonder if they're real?"

He put both hands on Moira Stevens' breasts and squeezed them cruelly. The next moment he let out a startled obscenity and took a quick step backward, as her nails raked down the side of his face.

"Who are these apes?" the brunette hissed.

"Alexei DuPlessis and Hank Sheppard," I said.

"You stupid bitch!" Sheppard snarled. "I'll rearrange your face and—"

He suddenly became very still as the barrel of Hicks's gun pressed tight against the side of his head.

"Relax," DuPlessis said, in a contemptuous voice. "If you want her that bad, Hank, maybe we can persuade Donavan to throw her into the pot as some kind of a bonus."

"Give me the gun," Moira Stevens said to Hicks, "and I'll kill the both of them right now!"

"Good-bye, gentlemen," I said.

"You hear that, Hank?" DuPlessis laughed shortly. "It takes a gentleman to recognize another gentleman. Did you know that?" He started toward the door. "Don't worry about the dummy. He's not about to do anything until his master tells him."

Hicks removed the gunbarrel from the side of Sheppard's head. For a long moment they just looked at each other, then Sheppard turned away and followed DuPlessis out of the room. The door closed behind them, and Moira Stevens exploded.

"You had the both of them here and you let them just walk away?" She looked at me like I was something that had just spilled out of the garbage can. "If he'd given me the gun, I would have killed them, and the hell with the consequences!" She looked at Hicks, and something flickered in the back of her eyes. "You would have killed them, too. Wouldn't you?"

"That's right," Hicks said expressionlessly.

She looked back at me. "When it comes right down to it, you're a goddamned spineless rabbit!" she said. "You don't have any guts at all, Donavan. You're useless!"

"He's got his reasons," Hicks said.

"Don't apologize for him," she said tightly. "I appreciate your loyalty, but it turns my stomach just to look at him right now." She put both her hands on his shoulders, then slowly ran them down his chest. "There's only one way I know to get rid of this fury inside me," she said softly. "You want to help me?"

Hicks looked down at her, his face still expressionless. "I don't see why not."

"I'm glad you're not a fag, or impotent, or whatever the hell it is that makes Donavan useless," she said. "Let's go to my room—now."

She tucked her arm through his possessively, and they walked toward the door. The hell with her, I thought. It would take a lot more than a few cheap gibes to make me annoyed. The door closed behind them, and I thought I might as well have another drink. It was just an infuriating coincidence that I happened to slam my knee into the side of a chair, so I fell off-balance heavily against the bar, and my arm just happened to sweep off the bottles and glasses on the bartop onto the floor. It could have happened to anybody.

CHAPTER NINE

Finchley called me from the hotel lobby, and I told him it was fine to send my visitor straight up to the suite. He arrived a couple of minutes later and I had a drink waiting for him, with no ice, of course.

"You're getting to be like a bad penny, Mr. Pace," I said, as I handed him the drink.

"But perhaps turning up in the nick of time?" He sat down on the couch, and cradled his drink in both hands. "How is the beautiful Miss Delato?"

"Kidnapped," I said.

He sighed gently. "You're beginning to disappoint me, Mr. Donavan. I had great faith in you, right from the beginning, from the way you successfully withstood the attempts on your life in New York. But now?"

"You didn't come here just to tell me about your disappointment in me."

"No, but I thought it was worth mentioning." He drank some of his drink. "The trouble is, Mr. Donavan, I can't afford for you to make any mistakes in this. My masters are pressing me for a definite answer. They want to know who it was—DuPlessis and his friends, or Donavan—who sabotaged the shipment. They're getting—well—restive isn't too strong a word."

"You mean your neck is on the block as well as mine?" I asked mildly.

"It's an unfortunate choice of phrase." He grimaced sharply. "But I suppose you could put it like that."

"DuPlessis has the girl," I said. "I can't risk her being harmed."

"Quixotic!" He shook his head slowly. "Don't go soft on me now, Donavan! Neither of us can afford it."

"I have a deal set up for the day after tomorrow," I said. "They want money in return for the girl. They can have their money. When I get the girl back, things will be different."

"They want the money, they want the girl, and they want you dead," he said irritably. "But not necessarily in that order." He finished his drink and held his glass out toward me.

"Help yourself," I said, and nodded toward the bar.

He flushed slightly, then got up and went over to the bar. "Your ex-help," he said. "The two chums who took the sea voyage with you. What are their names again?"

"Travers and Dryden," I said.

"Have you made contact with them yet?"

"They've disappeared," I said.

He carried his fresh drink back to the couch and sat down again. "They're with DuPlessis and Sheppard," he said. "It's been quite an exhausting week, you know? Keeping tabs on both sides, I mean. And expensive! Even the private detective agencies are getting quite grandiose ideas about their own worth."

"Travers and Dryden are with DuPlessis?" I said.

"They probably didn't have much choice," he said moodily. "I expect DuPlessis put it to them that if they were innocent of sabotage, they should prove it by helping him give you your comeuppance. I expect he's paying them quite generously, too."

"If you know this much," I said, "maybe you also know where I can find them."

"I thought you'd never ask." He sniffed irritably. "Miss Delato was staying with friends at a place called Little Chalmouth, and DuPlessis had her watched very carefully the whole time, until he picked the right moment to kidnap her. He's renting a farmhouse about ten miles away. The property is a little dilapidated, but it suits his purpose admirably because it's very isolated. Tucked away in a little valley, with only one access road—which isn't a road at all, really, not in the accepted sense of the word."

"How do I find him?"

"No problem." He got up, moved across to the desk against the wall, and helped himself to some of the hotel's stationery. "I'll draw you a map."

I walked across and watched over his shoulder until the map was completed.

"There you are," Pace said a couple of minutes later. "You make a right turn at the crossroads beyond Little Chalmouth and follow it for five miles. A lefthand turn, another couple of miles, and then you take the left fork which finally runs down into Manor End. The track that leads down to the farmhouse is about a mile before you reach the village, off to your right. It's very isolated country around there. I mean, they would hear a car turning in off the road, and I'm sure the farmhouse is well-guarded at all times."

"Thank you," I said.

He got up from the desk and moved back to the couch, then finished his drink and held the empty glass out toward me. "I'll have one more, if you don't mind," he said affably.

I hesitated for a long moment, then took the glass out of his hand. He watched with a contented smile while I made him a fresh drink, then brought it back to him.

"Thank you, dear boy," he said. "How you achieve it is up to you, of course. But please remember one thing. I must have the name of the man who hired DuPlessis to do the sabotage in the first place. Needless to say, the name will have to make sense to my masters. It would be useless for you to invent one. It has to be the *right* name, you understand?"

"I understand," I said.

"Good, good!" He sipped some of his drink,

then nodded. "It's a funny thing but this drink tastes so much better than the last. Perhaps because it was made with your own fair hand, as it were?"

"Perhaps," I said, and stifled a strong urge to hit him across the mouth.

"I can't make this point too strongly, Donavan," he said. "You must give me the right name. If you tell me the wrong name—something you've invented yourself—or if you tell me unfortunately DuPlessis was killed before you obtained the name, I shall have to presume it was you all along who sabotaged the shipment, and believe in DuPlessis' posthumous innocence. And the moment I tell my masters that, it will mean you won't have long to live."

"You have a gift for making yourself perfectly clear," I assured him.

"I'm so glad," he said.

"Like you said in New York, it was a tribal situation," I said. "We gave the guns to the Imroda who were rebelling against the majority tribe, the Nkria, who control the government. Isn't it possible the Nkria paid DuPlessis to do the sabotage?"

"My dear boy!" Pace rolled his eyes expressively. "You can't be that naïve! If the Nkria had been aware you were going to land a whole shipment of guns to help the Imroda revolt against them, don't you think they would have organized a welcoming party to await your landing?"

"You're right," I acknowledged. "It was stupid of me."

"Anyway," he said, "I don't know what you intend to do about DuPlessis and I don't want to know. All I want is the right name. When should I get in touch with you again?"

"Give me a couple of days," I told him. "Something's sure to have happened by then."

"I shall be very glad when it's all over," he said. "Frankly, my masters are becoming very touchy about the whole subject. Demanding, even, isn't too strong a word."

He finished his drink and got up onto his feet. "I wish you luck, Donavan."

"Thank you, Everard," I said.

It was around twenty minutes later, after Pace had left, when there was a brief knock on the door. Hicks and Moira Stevens walked into the room. She walked very slowly and stiffly, putting one leg carefully in front of the other, and hugged herself tight with both arms like she was scared she was about to fall apart.

"Tell him," Hicks said.

Her face was a dirty gray color, and her eyes were dark-ringed and heavy with fatigue as she looked at me.

"Tell him!" Hicks rapped.

Her face stiffened. "I just wanted to apologize," she muttered. "I'm sorry for all those horrible things I said about you."

"*Mister* Donavan," Hicks insisted.

Her teeth sank hard into her lower lip, then she

just managed to speak again. "Mister Donavan," she said obediently.

"It's real nice of you to make a voluntary apology," I said.

She looked at Hicks. "Can I go now?"

"Why not?" he said generously.

She turned around and walked out of the room slowly, dragging one foot after the other. Hicks moved across to the bar and made himself a drink, a faint self-satisfied grin on his face. I checked my watch.

"It's over three hours since the both of you disappeared," I said. "Not even a coffee-break?"

Hicks grinned. "I've been a long time without it, mate! She's more like a sprinter. Doesn't have the stamina for a marathon session!"

"The apology wasn't necessary," I said.

"It wasn't for you," he said good-humoredly. "It's what they call establishing a psychological advantage, right? If she don't do what I tell her to do, she gets hurt. So, the first time, you tell her to do something that's about the last bloody thing she wants to do. Then you make her do it. The second time around it's a hell of a lot easier."

"You're a ripe bastard, Hicks," I told him.

"So is she, mate," he said easily. "But a smashing pair of tits!"

"Pace was here." I told him what had been said and he got so interested, he even forgot about his drink for a few minutes.

"You think he was telling the truth?" he asked, when I had finished.

"I think so," I said.

"What are you going to do about it?"

"Buy a second-hand Range Rover in the morning," I said. "So we can drive up hill and down dale without having to stay on roads the whole time. Then we'll stock it from the armory in the basement and go take a look at that farmhouse."

"Right." His face brightened a little. "That sounds more like it. The way you just stood there and let those two bastards shoot off their mouths, I had a nasty feeling you were going soft on me for a moment."

"It's all this easy living," I said gravely. "I should get back to the jungle for a while."

"When the bleeding hell were you last in the jungle, mate?" Hicks snorted.

"1968," I said promptly. "It was a champagne safari, and I blooded my first movie camera."

"Bloody hilarious!" he snarled.

"You have any sentimental feelings toward Moira Stevens?" I asked him. "Post-coital triste, or anything like that?"

"You've got to be joking, mate!" He stared at me incredulously. "She wanted to get screwed, and I screwed her more than she wanted. It was as simple as that."

"She did look exhausted," I remembered.

"She was!"

"Probably went straight to bed?"

"She was worn out," Hicks said happily. "Poor bitch!"

"So now might be a good time to disturb her?" I said.

"What are you on about now?" He eyed me suspiciously. "Didn't you have enough last night—skating on that bloody water-bed—to last you for a couple of days?"

"Let's go," I said.

He finished his drink with one frantic gulp, then followed me out of the room. I tried the doorknob of Moira Stevens' room gently and found it was locked. It took a couple of minutes for Hicks to collect a spare key from Finchley and return with it. I unlocked the door and we walked quietly into the room. The drapes were tight-drawn, closing the last remnants of the twilight outside, and a peaceful hump in the bed showed the brunette was fast asleep. I closed the door in back of us, locked it, and slipped the key into my hip pocket. Then I turned on all the lights. Moira Stevens made a protesting grunt and pulled the covers over her head.

"Get her into the bathroom," I said.

Hicks stared at me blankly. "What for?" he asked.

"Just do as I say," I said impatiently.

"All right," he said grudgingly.

He walked over to the bed, shook the girl's arm gently, and said, "Wake up."

She made another protesting grunt and rolled over onto her stomach.

"You don't have the right technique," I told him.

I got hold of the covers and yanked them down to the foot of the bed. Then I slapped the suddenly-revealed ripe bottom with resounding force. Moira Stevens' body arched in protest and she let out a resounding shriek. I grabbed hold of her wrist and pulled her off the bed onto the floor.

"What—?" She blinked up at me, her face white with fury, then scrambled up onto her feet. "What the hell do you think you're doing?"

"We're going to talk," I said, "but not here. In the bathroom."

"You're crazy!" she snarled. "I could kill you for what you just did. Who the hell do you think you are, busting in—"

It was no time for argument. I sank my fingers into the thick bush of curly black pubic hair that nestled between the tops of her long tapering legs, took a tight grip, then started walking toward the bathroom. She let out another frantic scream, then came with me because she didn't have too much of a choice. I let go my grip when I had the glass door of the shower stall open, put the flat of my hand against her stomach, and pushed her inside. By that time she was sobbing with outrage and fury, and I didn't figure I would get much sense out of her until she had cooled off. I reached out behind her, turned the cold faucet on at full force and held her there with one hand. The sleeve of my coat was getting saturated, but I figured we all have to make some sacrifices. I let it run for maybe a couple of minutes, and by that time she had stopped struggling and trying to get out from under. When I turned off the faucet, she just stood there shivering uncontrollably. Her hair was a sodden mass, plastered tight to her scalp, and a skinned cat would have looked happier by comparison.

"We're going to talk," I said. "All I want from you is an answer when I ask a question. No screams, no abuse. You understand?"

"Get fucked!" she said thinly.

I turned the cold faucet on at full blast again, and held her under it for another minute. When I turned off the faucet, her lips had a blue look about them.

"You know what hearsay evidence is?" I asked her.

"No," she muttered, and tried to stop her teeth chattering.

"It's when somebody tells you something, and you accept it without proof," I said. "Like when you told me you were Madden's sister."

"I was," she said.

"Somebody wanted to get me vitally interested in DuPlessis and Sheppard," I said, "and you helped them. You told me in the bar, you'd thought about it a lot. How to pique my curiosity."

"You're mad," she said, in a sullen voice. "I nearly got killed a couple of times just by being with you."

"I don't think so," I said. "Whoever hired the guns didn't want me to get killed. They wanted me to be scared enough to think I could get killed."

"What about that first time in the bar? If you hadn't had your gorilla planted there already, that man would have shot the both of us!"

"My guess is he would have fired and missed, or fired a couple of blanks and then run," I said. "But that's hindsight. At the time I was very relieved when Hicks blew off the back of his head. The thing is, only two people knew we were going to be in that bar at a certain time—you and me. And *I* didn't tell him, for sure. It's the same when the guy in the car took a shot at us when we were leaving the penthouse. That time, only three of us knew I was going to be there—you, me, and Madden. Again, I didn't tell him, and I don't think Madden told him, because Madden got himself murdered the next night."

"You're mad!" she said tiredly.

"Somebody hired Madden to pretend he'd been in the plot, along with DuPlessis and Sheppard, to kill me for revenge," I said. "Then his story was he decided he preferred to get rich by selling me the information because money was preferable to revenge. But somewhere along the way he changed his mind and called me. You overheard the conversation—or listened-in on an extension—and told your boss. He decided the only way out was to have Madden killed, and fast. So he did, but his help didn't get away in time before we arrived."

She shivered again, even more violently. "Please let me out of here!" she whimpered. "I'll freeze to death!"

"We've only just started," I assured her. "Your boss put you alongside Madden because he didn't trust him. Madden was promised a lot of money, but something made him change his mind and that's why he was killed. But when we arrived at the front door you did some fast thinking. You got one of them to grab hold of you and use you as a shield. It was obvious that all they wanted to do was get the hell out of there, and they would have, except for you. You knew that you couldn't afford to have them keep on living, because the chances were we'd get around to asking them some questions and they might very well come up with the right answers. So you screamed out that they'd killed Madden, and that did it up just fine for them. That story about how they were about to rape you when we arrived had a touch of genius about it. My guess is, if there was any rape involved, they were about to be the victims."

"I just don't know what you're talking about," she whimpered. "I'm going to die if you keep me standing here!"

"You know the thing that makes me really mad?" I asked, in a soft voice. "Tamara."

"Tamara?" Her head jerked up and she looked at me blankly. "Who in hell is Tamara?"

"Speak softly of the dead," I told her, and backhanded her across the mouth. "Tamara was a very dear friend of mine. The time you invited me over to the penthouse to talk with Madden, I left Tamara alone in the hotel suite. You and your boss knew exactly where I was, so it made things very easy for somebody to get into the suite and strangle her to death."

"I don't know anything about that," she said quickly. "I swear it!"

"All I want is the name of your boss," I said, "partner, or whatever the hell he is. I'll give you five seconds to tell me, and if you don't, I'm going to turn on the hot faucet." I held out both hands in front of her face. "I have very strong wrists. I'll keep turning the faucet until it breaks off in my hand. Then I'll close the glass door and keep it shut. That'll leave you inside, with no way to turn off the hot water, which will keep on getting hotter. It's an easy choice, Moira. You can tell me now, or you can stay here and scald to death."

"I honestly have no idea what you're talking about!" she said.

"That leaves you another couple of seconds," I said.

"You can't!" Her eyes stared fiercely into mine. "You wouldn't!"

I reached past her with one hand and turned on the hot faucet, and kept turning it.

"No!" She tried to get past me, in a frantic surge of energy, and I pushed her back with the flat of my hand.

The faucet reached the point of no return. I waited for a moment, then gave it a sharp wrench. There was a snapping sound and it came away in my hand. I let it drop onto the tiled floor of the shower stall, took a couple of steps backward, then swung the glass door shut.

"Good-bye, Moira Stevens," I said.

Steam started to fill the bathroom as her fists hammered hysterically on the glass door. Hicks looked at me with an expression close to wonder in his eyes, opened his mouth to say something, then thought better of it and closed it again. She began to scream, and it wasn't the most pleasant sound in the world. I held the door tight shut and figured the glass was too strong for her fists to break it.

"All right!" she screamed, maybe a half-minute later. "I'll tell you, but for God's sake let me out of here!"

"Give me the name first," I said, "and make sure it's the right one the first time. You won't get a second chance."

"Goddamn you to hell!" she yelled, and then she suddenly started to make choking sounds. "Pace!" she screamed, with sudden clarity.

"Who?" I said.

"Everard Pace. Pace! Pace!"

There was a soggy kind of noise as she fell onto the floor. I opened the glass door, slid my hands under her armpits and pulled her out of the stall. She lay limply on the tiled floor, her flesh a bright, broiled-looking pink, but no worse than that.

"I suppose you'd better do something for her," I said to Hicks. "Then put her back into bed and disconnect the phone." I took the key out of my hip pocket. "Lock her in here when you've finished. And I guess you'd better get Finchley to do something about all that hot water going to waste."

CHAPTER TEN

"Everlasting cock-stand Pace!" Hicks said, after he had made himself a drink. "I should have known, just by the look of the bastard!"

"Is everything under control?" I asked politely.

"I dried her off, rubbed her all over with a salve, and put her back to bed," he said. "She started getting hysterical again, so I gave her a half-pint of neat brandy. That seemed to do the trick. She was sleeping like a babe when I left the room."

"Not badly burned?"

He shook his head. "She's going to feel bleeding tender for a few days. But if you mean does she need a doctor, no, she doesn't."

"You locked the door?"

"Do me a favor!" he sighed. "Yes, I locked the door, ripped out the phone cord, and Finchley's got one of his night porters standing guard outside her room. He thinks she's a nut-case, and the first moment he hears anything unusual going on—like a window breaking—he's going to call me."

"I know I shouldn't have asked," I said generously.

"What about Pace?"

"He'll keep," I said. "We're going to get back Francine Delato first."

"A nice day out in the country," he said cheerfully. "I think I'd like that."

"Suppose we use tear gas?"

"You'd never get close enough, mate," he said. "Not with four pros like them inside the house. If the girl wasn't inside, I'd say we could use a bazooka and blow the four of them to buggery, or beyond."

"So we'll have to get Francine out first," I said. "You have any ideas about how?"

"No." He sighed heavily. "But I can see I'm going to have to think about it for the rest of the bleeding night." He shot me a dark look, full of suspicion. "How long have you known about them? Pace and the Stevens bitch, I mean?"

"Since just before we left New York," I said. "Maybe earlier."

"Why didn't you do something about it before this, then?"

"Because we weren't supposed to," I said. "We were supposed to be worried because we didn't know what the hell was happening. Pace had to convince us the threat from DuPlessis and Sheppard was for real."

"He did that all right," he grunted. "What if she hadn't told you his name?"

"She would have scalded to death," I said.

"You bloody well mean that?"

"I think so," I said honestly. "I'm almost sure I did at the time."

"You're a cold-blooded bastard most of the time," he said, in a brooding voice. "Then, other times, you can get bleeding soppily sentimental. My trouble is, I'm never quite sure which mood you're bloody well in at any given moment!"

"Pick up the secondhand Range Rover as soon as you can in the morning," I said, "and get hold of a large-scale ordinance map of the district. I'll tell Finchley to let you have what you want from the armory. Get me a submachinegun—a Mark Five Sten will do just fine. You'll need an automatic rifle with a powerful scope. And anything else you figure necessary. I'll be back for an early lunch tomorrow, and we'll get going after that. Just one more thing. Don't let Moira Stevens do anything stupid, like get away from the hotel, right?"

"You're going out?"

"Right," I agreed.

"Back to that nympho bird?" He shook his head bleakly. "That's about all you need right now, mate. Another bash on the head!"

Fifteen minutes later I stood outside the town house in Knightsbridge and pressed the button beside the name Delato.

"Hello?" a tinny voice said through the entry phone.

"Is that the Florence Nightingale of the waterbed set?" I asked politely.

There was a rich gurgle of laughter, then the

buzzer rasped, and I pushed the front door open. When I reached the second floor, the front door of the flat was open, and Angela Hartford was waiting for me.

"I hoped you'd come and see me tonight, Paul," she said, "but then I thought you probably had a dreadful headache and had gone to bed with an aspirin, or something equally uninspiring!"

She was ideally dressed for the short hot English summer, wearing a white halter-top and hipster pants in a crazy floral design. Her navel gave me a broad wink the moment before I shifted my focus back to her face.

"Come on in and I'll get you a Scotch on the rocks," she said.

"Make me a Scotch on the rocks," I corrected her. "We must keep our idiom right."

I walked into the living room, and the huge aspidistra plant maintained a baleful silence. Angela came back into the room a few seconds later and gave me my drink.

"Do you want anything to eat?" she asked anxiously. "I make a wonderful fish dish with a shrimp sauce. It comes in a plastic bag, and you shove it into boiling water for twenty minutes."

"I've eaten, thanks," I said, and shuddered gently.

"I haven't heard anything from Francine," she said. "Have you, by any chance?"

"She's still in the country, I heard," I told her. "But staying with different people now."

"She could have given me a ring!" Angela

shrugged her shoulders. "Oh, well, that's the Italians for you, and I'm only her best friend! Do you like opera, Paul?"

"It's okay," I said cautiously.

"I like it, too. That's the trouble, you see? If nobody liked opera, we wouldn't need Italians."

I drank some of my drink, because it saved me the trouble of trying to dream up an answer.

"Did you have an intellectual relationship with Francine?" Angela asked casually.

"Not exactly," I admitted.

"Purely sexual?" Her voice had a satisfied note to it. "Do it whenever you could, eh?"

"I guess so," I said, and choked slightly on a mouthful of Scotch.

"I'm so glad," she said. "I mean, it was obvious from the very beginning our relationship was going to be purely sexual—or impurely sexual?—and I would have felt left out of things if you'd had an intellectual relationship with Francine as well. I tried reading a D. H. Lawrence novel once, but the dirty bits were too few and far between, if you know what I mean."

"How about Henry Miller?" I suggested.

"I've never met him," she said innocently. "What does he do?"

"It doesn't seem important right now," I said.

"I had this dreadful nightmare after you left last night," she said. "It made me cry! I dreamed, instead of hitting your head against the wall, you somehow turned sideways while you were skidding along the water bed so—"

"I don't think I want to know," I said quickly.

"It's such a beautiful ding-dong, Paul," she said, "and, in my nightmare, I just knew it would never be the same afterward!"

"Let's talk about something else," I said desperately. "How's your peeping tom across the street?"

"I almost forgot about him." She walked across to the window and stood there looking out. "It's time to say good night." She pulled off the white halter-top and waved it brightly for a few seconds, then dropped it to the floor. I watched fascinated, as she pulled the heavy drapes tight shut, then turned around toward me. Her magnificent breasts bounced gently as she came back toward me.

"That should send him to bed in a frenzy," she said complacently. "Why don't you take off your clothes, Paul?"

"Why not?" I agreed.

"Would you like another drink?"

"Sure," I said.

She took the glass from me and disappeared in the direction of the kitchen. I got out of my clothes and sat down on the couch. The chintzy velvet against my bare skin made me itch. Angela came back into the room, gave me my fresh drink, and nodded her approval.

"That's much better, sweetie. Now you look relaxed." She leaned forward to take a closer look, and her full breasts spilled gently into my face. "Too relaxed! The sight of me even half-naked should drive you out of your mind with berserk passion, didn't you know that?" Her fingers played a short etude, and it was the work of a virtuoso. "That's better," she said. "Now it's got some ding into its lovely dong."

She straightened up again, stripped off the hipster pants, and the brief briefs she was wearing underneath.

"I don't think the water bed was an unqualified success, do you?" she said.

"No." I fingered the bruise on my forehead tenderly.

"There is a bed in my bedroom, of course," she went on, "but it's only a single bed, and it wouldn't be any use to a couple of big people like us. I mean, it might be all right for a couple of midgets, but I just don't think it would stand up to all that bouncing when we got going. And I hate knee-tremblers!"

"Knee-tremblers?" I had to ask.

"When you do it standing up," she explained. "The last time I ever did that I was only about eighteen, and we were doing it on the front porch of my parents' house in the country. We were just working up to a climax when my father opened the front door to put the cat out. Well, there I was, rear-view, with my dress hiked up around my waist and my pants down around my knees. He nearly put me out along with the cat!"

I pulled my drink down on the small table, got up onto my feet, then pulled the cushions off the couch and the armchairs, and carefully grouped them on the rug.

"That's a brilliant idea," she said. "I mean, there's almost no chance of you falling through the floor, is there?"

I jackknifed forward from the waist, caught hold of her nearest leg behind the knee, and jerked it upward. The next moment she was sprawling on her back on the cushions.

"How masterful!" she purred. "But don't you dare dive on top of me, or you'll wind up with splinters in your ding-dong!"

I lay down beside her and began a gentle and intimate exploration of her body with both hands. After a little while she began to purr audibly, and responded in kind. A kiss is still a kiss, wherever it's delivered, and things rapidly progressed to a situation where they had been delivered just about everyplace.

The beast with two backs was how some unimaginative anti-sex fiend once described it, and we disproved his image with no trouble at all. And then, a long time later, when the tumultuous climax had quietened to a sense of sweet satiation, we lay side by side on the cushions and I began to realize they were still just as itchy as they had ever been.

"I know," Angela said lazily. "It's horrible, isn't it?" She turned away from me onto her side. "Scratch my bottom for me, duckie?" I duly obliged and she purred her thanks. "I'm sorry I don't have any champagne tonight," she apologized.

"Never mind," I told her.

I came up into a sitting position and rescued my Scotch from the small table. The lone ice cube had long before dissolved, but I was cast in the same mold as my pioneer ancestors and built to withstand hardship with fortitude.

"Sweetie?" Angela struggled up into a sitting position and looked at me earnestly. "What are we going to do when Francine gets back?"

"I hadn't thought about it," I said honestly.

"I suppose there must be some kind of social etiquette that applies in a situation like this." She wrinkled her nose thoughtfully. "I mean, does Francine have a prior right to your services because she knew you first?"

"I wouldn't have any idea," I said.

"Are you going to be here long?" she asked. "In England, I mean?"

"It depends," I said.

"There's an awful lot of things you aren't sure about, Paul," she said, in a disapproving voice. "I was thinking, if you were going to stay here for a while, we could share you turnabout, you know."

"How long I stay depends on tomorrow, mostly," I told her.

"Perhaps we'd better make the most of tonight and not worry about tomorrow," she said. "You *are* going to stay for the rest of the night?"

"You're damned right I am," I told her, then finished my drink and put the glass back on the table.

"Good," she purred. "How is your ding-dong now?" Her fingers deftly checked out the situation. "Still sluggish." She sighed. "I suppose you might as well have another drink."

"I'll get it," I said.

"Oh, no!" She got up onto her feet quickly. "I'll get it. You'll only trip over something and break your leg, or something dreadful."

"Don't be stupid!" I said tersely.

"Sweetie!" She looked down at me, her china blue eyes openly commiserating. "You're accident-prone. Didn't you know?"

"I am not accident-prone!" I said, from between clenched teeth.

"You are so!" she said hotly. "I thought you'd killed yourself last night when you crashed your head into the wall."

"It was the kind of accident that could have happened to anybody," I said firmly.

"You were unconscious for at least five minutes," she said, then giggled suddenly.

"What's so goddamned funny about that?" I growled.

"I suddenly remembered," she said, and giggled again. "You still had that lovely big erection the whole time you were out cold. That's why I couldn't bring myself to call a doctor. I mean, of course everybody's heard of death in ecstasy, but that would have looked ridiculous!"

"Just get me the drink," I snarled.

She leaned across me to pick up the glass, the tips of her breasts just resting on my head, and the temptation was irresistible. I slid my hand quickly up between her legs and gave the honey-

colored fuzz that nestled there a sharp tug. She
let out a sharp yelp of surprise and jumped violently. One foot hit the edge of a cushion and
skidded, throwing her off-balance. She let out another yelp as she fell forward, her legs stradling
my shoulders so that for a giddy moment there, I
was suddenly wearing a honey-colored beard.
Then her unexpected weight knocked me backward onto the cushions, and the momentum carried her further forward so she skidded on her
front across the tabletop, and crashed to the floor
the other side.

I was going to get up and help her but I
couldn't, because I was laughing too much. The
laughter welled up inside me and exploded in my
throat. I laughed until my stomach ached unmerci-
fully and my fists drummed the cushions. Then, finally, I slowly realized she was standing over me
again, her clenched fists resting on her hips, and
her face threatening bloody murder.

"You stupid sod!" she said thickly. "I could
have got killed! What the bloody hell is so funny
about that?"

"Nothing," I agreed, "and it was all my fault,
Angela. I should have gone and gotten the drink
in the first place. I mean"—my shoulders started to
shake again helplessly—"after all, we both know
you're accident-prone!"

For a nasty moment there, I figured she was
about to stomp me to death with her bare feet.
But then she slowly turned away and walked out
of the room, muttering darkly to herself. She came

back a couple of minutes later, carrying a drink in each hand.

"I was going to grab a kitchen knife and slit your throat from ear to ear," she said nastily. "But then I thought you just weren't worth it, so I decided to have a drink instead."

She sat down beside me on the cushions, and took a cautious sip of her drink. "I'm sore and bruised," she said accusingly, "and if that glass had broken I could have been maimed for life, or worse!"

"But it didn't break, did it?" I said comfortingly.

"You were really horrid to me, Paul," she said, in a severe voice. "I feel very hurt and not loving at all, and you're going to have to make it up to me."

"You're right," I said soberly. "How would you like a nice day in the country?"

CHAPTER ELEVEN

The Range Rover was parked beside a thick clump of tall trees, around five hundred yards from the nearest dirt road. The sun was shining brightly from a clear blue sky and dappling the lush leaves with glorious color. A bumblebee, drunk with pollen, banged into the windshield and slid down onto the hood so it landed on its back and waved its legs feebly at us. We were probably trespassing, but it wasn't a thought to upset me right then.

Hicks and myself were wearing faded blue coveralls and could have been mechanics from some local garage. Angela was wearing a white cotton shirt and old corduroy pants. With her blond hair streaming down over her shoulders, and no makeup, she looked the typical kind of upper—class English girl who likes to help Daddy out on the farm by exercizing the horses and laying the farmhands in the stable.

"What's the time?" Hicks asked.

I checked my watch. "Ten of five."

"You sure you don't want to wait longer?" he

said. "The light will hold until around nine, anyway, and it won't be dark before ten."

"They figure they've got everything sewn up real neat," I said. "They're going to meet us at the local pub at noon tomorrow, and we'll have all that lovely money with us. It's a nice lazy afternoon and, with any luck, maybe a couple of them are having a siesta."

"Maybe," he said, with no enthusiasm at all. "There's a ditch that runs down the edge of that field on the top slope. I can get to the end of it with no sweat, but that's as far as I can get. Should give me a range of three hundred yards. No problem with the scope. Give me twenty minutes to get into position before you start out, okay?"

"Sure," I said.

"It's a nice quiet afternoon," he went on. "So I'll hear the motor."

"Ninety seconds after it stops," I said. "No longer."

"Ninety seconds, mate. If it works out all right, send the girl out the back door where I can see her. If she's not there in three minutes after I open up, I'm coming in."

Hicks got out of the Range Rover, walked around to the back, and opened the doors. He took out the FN automatic rifle, scope, and bipod, and put them carefully on the ground. Then he closed the doors again.

"I've got a couple of spare magazines with me," he said. He carefully attached the scope and the bipod to the gun, then picked it up and slung it over his shoulder. "Just one thing, mate," he said carefully. "Don't go getting excited, right?"

"I never get excited," I said coldly.

"It's moments like these I wish I'd been what my old mum wanted me to be," he said bitterly. "A bleeding porter at Smithfield's meat market."

He started walking and was soon lost in the thick clump of trees. I checked my watch again, then lighted a small cigar. The bumblebee made a supreme effort and righted itself, then droned off aimlessly. Somewhere above our heads a couple of birds started chattering about the state of the country.

"I feel a little nervous," Angela confessed. "Do you feel nervous, Paul?"

"I never feel nervous," I told her. "Mainly because I get to feeling scared before I get the chance to feel nervous."

"I'm not so much scared, as shit-scared," she said.

"Do you want a drink?" I asked. "There's a flask of brandy in the back."

"I don't think so, thanks," she said.

"I'd like to say you can still back out of it," I said. "But it's too late now."

"I know." She nodded slowly. "But you were honest about it before I agreed to do it."

"You should be okay," I said. "You know what to do?"

"I drive right up to the farmhouse and stop, so

the car's facing the front door," she recited. "I switch off the motor and get out."

"Fast," I said. "They'll have heard us coming, and they'll have a reception committee waiting for us."

"It's all right, Paul." She gave me a wan smile. "I won't let you down. Don't forget, I'm still Francine's best friend."

"Leave us hope I prove to be the best friend of the both of you," I muttered.

The minutes dragged by slowly. Then, at last, it was time to start out. I drove the Range Rover back onto the dirt road, and then the half mile to where it joined up with the road that ran past the front of the farmhouse. I stopped just before the junction and walked around to the back, while Angela moved into the driver's seat. I opened the doors, climbed into the back, and carefully closed the doors again. The Sten was there, the magazine already in place. I lay down on the floor of the Range Rover, facing the doors, and held the Sten in my hands. Angela started the motor and we moved forward again.

"I'm turning into the driveway now," she said, a couple of minutes later.

I turned the cocking handle out of the safety slot of the gun and pushed the button marked "R" from the left-hand side, so I would get one shot each time I pulled the trigger. If you push the button from the other side marked "A," you get automatic fire. That's one thing I like about a Sten, it allows you to change your mind real fast.

"I'm about fifty yards from the house now," Angela said, in a brittle-sounding voice. "The front door's opening ... a man's coming out ... he's waving for me to stop."

"Give him a bright smile," I said, "and keep on going, but don't hurry."

The car came to a stop a moment later, and the motor died.

"Good afternoon!" Angela's voice sounded fraudulently bright and cheerful. "I wonder if you could help me?" The door slammed shut in back of her. "I'm looking for a friend of mine, Francine Delato. Everard Pace told me she was staying with you. I mean, you are Mr. DuPlessis, are you not? Everard said he was sure Francine would be with you for the next few days, at least, and it's quite urgent I contact her, actually, so—"

I undid the back doors of the Range Rover and gently pushed them open, then slid my feet down onto the ground.

"Who the hell are you?" Sheppard's voice asked, thick with suspicion.

"Angela Hartford. I expect Francine's mentioned my name? I'm her best friend, actually, and we share a flat in—"

"Come inside," Sheppard grunted, "and we'll talk about it."

There was a startled yelp from Angela, followed by a quick series of scuffling sounds. I risked a brief look around the side of the Range Rover. Sheppard had a fistful of the front of Angela's shirt bunched in his grasp and was pulling her back inside the house. A couple of moments later the front door slammed shut. It was about the only eventuality I had never goddamned well figured on!

There was a breaking sound as a pane of glass shattered in the main window along the low facade of the farmhouse, to the right of the front door. The next moment a rifle barrel emerged. I ducked frantically for cover as it started firing, and three shots ricocheted off the side of the Range Rover. There was a short and painful silence, and then the firing started again. But this time it was from a lot further away. The ninety seconds since the motor had stopped had elapsed, and Hicks had opened up on the back of the farmhouse.

So now the whole goddamned situation was desperate. Both girls were now inside the house. In less than three minutes Hicks would break cover and almost certainly be mown down before he could get anywhere near the back of the farmhouse. I had to do something, and do it fast. The adrenalin was pumping into my veins and I wasn't so much excited as frantic.

I pushed the "A" button on the right-hand side of the Sten, then took a convulsive leap that landed me about four feet clear of the back of the Range Rover. I fired a short burst into the shattered window and saw the rifle barrel abruptly disappear. There was no time to think. I took a quick run, then launched myself at the broken window with the Sten held out in front of my face. More glass shattered, and then I was inside. I landed with a breath-shattering thump on top of a large table, skidded along its surface, and fell off the other end. Somebody fired a couple of shots, and splinters from the wooden floor kicked up into the side of my face. I turned onto my side, swinging the Sten around, and saw Sheppard framed in a doorway with a gun in his hand. I fired another burst from the Sten, and it lifted him off his feet and sent him crashing backward into the hallway.

There was only one other occupant in the room I saw, as I scrambled onto my feet. Travers lay on his back in front of the broken window. The first burst I had fired from the Sten must have stitched a line of bullets across his chest. The front of his shirt was a whole mess of blood, and he was very dead. The sound of Hicks firing still continued steadily, with about a five-second interval between each shot.

I walked over to the doorway and looked out into the hall. Sheppard was also stretched out on his back, the new blood-red eye centered between the other two staring at me accusingly. I poked the barrel of the Sten out into the hallway, and somebody fired a couple of quick shots at it, so I retreated further back into the living room. Travers hadn't been a big guy, so it was no trick to pick him up with one hand by the scruff of the neck and haul him across to the doorway. I poked the barrel of the Sten out into the hallway again, followed by Travers' head at the approximate height my own head would have been, and had I been that goddamned stupid. There were another quick couple of shots. I screamed as convincingly as I could, pulled both the Sten and Travers' body back into the room, then let the body drop to the floor with a satisfactory thud.

The house seemed very quiet, except for the sound of Hicks's methodical firing. I retreated a couple of steps and flattened myself against the wall—pushed the "R" button on the left-hand side of the Sten, and waited. Maybe a minute later, I heard a faint sound from someplace outside in the hallway. Then, finally, Dryden's head appeared inside the doorway. He was holding a rifle in his hands, and I figured the chances of him dropping it if I told him to were remote. So I put a bullet into him. The rifle spilled out of his hands onto the floor, and he followed it soon after. I waited right where I was until I was satisfied there was nobody else outside in the hallway, then I moved closer and kneeled down beside him. The bullet had taken him through the side of the head. It was the kind of trick I wouldn't be able to pull twice, so I went out through the broken window as quietly as I could, and around the side of the farmhouse.

The farmhouse was a long, low, one-story building, maybe three hundred years old, and built of stone. That meant it didn't have too many windows, and I was grateful. I reached the back of it and stopped. There was a slight risk Hicks might shoot at me, but I was counting on his scope being powerful enough to recongize me. I sank down onto my knees, and poked my head cautiously around the corner. Hicks was still firing regularly. His next shot sent a small puff of powdered stone drifting in the still air, then a rifle barrel protruded through an open window and returned his shot. I pushed the button back to "A" on the Sten, straightened up onto my feet again, and took another of those convulsive leaps that were rapidly becoming my usual means of getting around. The leap brought me into a position almost facing the window, and as my feet touched the ground, I pulled the trigger of the Sten. I kept on firing until the magazine was empty, because I figured DuPlessis wasn't the kind of guy who would die easy. For a heart-stopping moment nothing happened, then his body came crashing through the window and fell onto the ground.

I turned around toward the slope of the hill and waved. A couple of seconds later Hicks emerged from the ditch and started moving toward me quickly.

"What about the others, then?" he asked, as he came up beside me.

"Dead," I told him.

"It worked all right, then?" He looked vaguely surprised. "Using the girl to throw them off-balance, I mean?"

"Sure," I said. "Well, kind of."

"Where are they?"

"I don't know," I said truthfully. "I was about to go take a look. See if you can find a pot of paint and a brush someplace, will you? Then bring them into the house."

The back door was locked, so I walked around to the front of the house and opened the front door. It still seemed very silent as I walked down the hallway.

"Angela?" I yelled. "Francine?"

"We're here," said a very nervous upper-class English accent. "Is it all right to come out now?"

"Sure," I said.

The both of them cautiously emerged from a room further down the hallway. Angela's face was slightly flushed and she looked breathless. Francine's clothes looked rumpled and dusty, but the rich beauty of her face and figure was still unimpaired.

"*Caro mio!*" she said, in her bubbling liquid accent. "I knew you would come and rescue me and kill those filthy swine!"

"We could never have done it without Angela," I said.

"They had her tied to a chair, and I had a dreadful time loosening the ropes," Angela said. "My nails are absolutely ruined!"

"And you have been unfaithful to me, darling!" Francine said, pouting at me. "Angela has confessed everything!"

"So we've made this arrangement," Angela said. "It seemed to be the fairest thing for both of us."

"Arrangement?"

"We thought you could hire a nice yacht in the Mediterranean," Angela said enthusiastically. "And we could go for a lovely long cruise, just the three of us."

"But no water bed," Francine said, then giggled hysterically. "Angela tells me you become a madman on a water bed!"

Hicks came into the hallway, carrying a pot of paint and a brush. "It's red," he said. "Will that do?"

"Just fine," I told him.

We went into the living room. I dipped the brush into the paint and wrote NKRIA in blood-red letters across the tabletop. Then I carefully wiped the handle of the brush clean with my pocket handkerchief and dropped the brush back into the paintpot.

"Maybe it will help confuse the issue," I said. "The four of them were mercenaries and all of them fought in Malagai in the revolt against the Nkria government. What do you bet that by tomorrow at least a half-dozen people who live around here will have seen mysterious black shapes slipping through the woods at night, the tips of their spears glistening in the moonlight?"

"You don't half bleeding well carry on!" Hicks said, in a morose voice.

CHAPTER TWELVE

Moira Stevens was sitting in a chair, wearing a thin robe and a pinched expression on her face. Hicks closed the door in back of us and locked it.

"How are you?" I asked politely.

"It's no thanks to you I'm still alive!" She moved her shoulders and winced. "My back is blistered all over!"

"How about the more interesting places?" Hicks asked.

"You're an insensitive bastard!" she told him.

"We're going visiting," I said. "Get some clothes on."

"I couldn't walk a step," she said flatly.

Hicks yanked her out of the chair, ripped off the robe, then spun her around so she was facing away from him. His hand delivered a tremendous slap that sounded like a thunderclap across her bottom and she went squealing across the room.

"You can walk all right," he said mildly, "and there's only one small blister on your back."

She got dressed slowly, in sullen silence, while the both of us watched her indifferently.

"Where are we going?" she asked, when she was finally ready.

"Visiting with Everard," I said. "I guess you know where we can find him?"

"He'll kill me!"

"We'll see he doesn't," I assured her.

"I won't go!"

"Did Finchley get that shower fixed?" I asked Hicks.

"This morning," he said.

"It's a shame." I shook my head slowly. "Now I'm going to have to bust it again."

"He lives in Bayswater," she said quickly. "I'll take you there."

The traffic through Hyde Park was heavy, and the ride from the hotel took about twenty minutes. Pace occupied a penthouse on the twelfth floor of an opulent apartment block. He opened the front door just after our second ring, and Hicks pushed a gun into his stomach. Then the four of us moved inside the apartment, into the living room with its strong Japanese influence in the furnishings and the faint smell of incense in the air.

"A bloody poof!" Hicks sniffed irritably. "Thought he was, the first time I saw the bleeding jerk!"

"I'd like to know what the hell this is all about!" Pace barked. "Will you kindly explain, Donavan?"

"Mission accomplished," I said. "We saw Du-Plessis today."

"You got the girl back unharmed?" His pale blue eyes watched my face intently.

"Unharmed," I agreed.

"I'm so glad," he said. "Would you care for a drink?"

"Not right now," I said. "I talked with Du-Plessis before he died."

"Really?"

"He gave me the name," I said. "The name you wanted to hear. The name your masters want to hear."

"Excellent!" He smiled briefly. "And the name?"

"Everard Pace," I said.

He looked at me, then at Hicks, then slowly back at me again. "What is this?" he asked. "Some kind of a bad joke?"

"You made a deal with the Malagaian government," I said. "You guaranteed that shipment of arms would be sabotaged before it was ever used against them. But you didn't dare sabotage it before it was placed on board the ship. It was guarded too closely by your own men, and you couldn't risk one of them seeing you and reporting it to your masters. So you needed an accomplice, DuPlessis. He was to sabotage the shipment after it had been landed, and he did. But afterwards he got to thinking why the hell should he split the payment with you? After all, he'd done all the work. So he told the Malagaians he had done all the work, and they paid him. Then he told you the sabotage had been done before the shipment was ever landed."

"I think you're mad, Donavan," he said. "Do you know that? You are stark raving mad!"

"It made for a lot of problems," I said. "If DuPlessis was telling the truth, then somebody on board the ship must have done it. I was the most obvious choice. Also, your masters were very upset about the whole thing, and demanding you find out who the culprit was, and deal with him. So you sold DuPlessis the idea that the only way he could prove his innocence was by killing me, and you set up that elaborate fiction in New York that DuPlessis was after my blood at the same time. You kept both sides well informed what the others were doing, and carefully built it up to a confrontation. You gave me the edge finally by telling me where I could find DuPlessis and the rest of them. You didn't honestly believe I had done it. Hell! It was me who had paid for the shipment in the first place. But you also made the fatal mistake of believing DuPlessis wasn't smart enough to have done it on his own. You figured there had to be somebody in back of him. Somebody you didn't know, and you wanted to know that name very badly. So badly, you handed me DuPlessis on a plate, just so I could get the name of the man who had cheated you out of being paid for the sabotage. So now you've got it: DuPlessis!"

"I still think you're a raving lunatic!" he said hotly.

"Dear Moira has confessed everything," I said,

"with just a little persuasion. There's something else that interests me very much, Everard. Did you kill Tamara personally, or did you just hire somebody to do it?"

"He would have done it himself," Moira Stevens said, in a dry brittle voice. "He's a sadist. He loves to hurt people. Killing somebody—especially a girl!—would be the ultimate kick for him."

Pace's mustache twitched briefly, then he pulled out a pocket handkerchief and gently dabbed his forehead. "Can't we talk this over, Donavan?" he said huskily. "I'm sure we can come to some arrangement that will be mutually satisfactory."

"I know your masters," I told him. "Well, two of them, anyway. I called Bouchard in Paris before we came to visit with you this evening, and told him everything."

His face turned a dirty gray color. "He wouldn't believe you," he said, but there was no conviction in his voice.

"I would be delighted to leave you in his capable hands," I said, "but there's the personal matter of Tamara's death. She was very dear to me."

"What are you going to do?" he muttered.

"Give me the gun," I told Hicks, and he handed it over.

I hefted it in my hand for a moment, then pointed the barrel at Pace's chest. "Why don't you turn your head away?" I suggested. "It might make things a little easier?"

For a moment there, he was about to start begging, but then he took another look at my face and changed his mind. He turned his head slowly, his shoulders hunching instinctively, and stared at the wall. I reversed my grip on the gun so I now held it by the barrel, and slammed the butt down across the back of his head. He slumped forward onto the floor and lay there without moving.

"Perhaps you would both care to wait in the front hall?" I suggested.

They went out of the room silently, and Hicks carefully closed the door in back of them. The French doors opened out onto a small balcony, complete with a line of potted plants all in their summer's array. I dragged Pace out onto the balcony, pushed him half-over it with his head hanging down, and waited until I was sure the street, twelve floors below, was clear. Then I got one arm under his knees, heaved, and he fell into Eternity.

"I didn't hear any shot, mate," Hicks said, as we rode the elevator back down.

"No," I agreed. "He had to step out for a moment, and I don't think he'll be back."

There was small knot of people gathered on the sidewalk in front of the apartment building, so we walked in the opposite direction to get a cab. Twenty minutes later we were back inside the hotel, and also back inside Moira Stevens' room. She sank down into an armchair, and looked at me almost pitifully.

"You killed him," she said. "I know you did, and you know I know you killed him. So what's going to happen to me now?"

"I've been thinking about that," Hicks said. "You're going to hire a bloody great yacht and go cruising in the Mediterranean, is that right, mate?"

"That's right," I said.

"You," he said, "and that Italian bird, and the blond with the big tits and the la-de-da accent. Bleeding lovely for you, but where does it leave me? Out in the shithouse, that's where! I'll do all the bleeding work and get none of the bleeding fun. So I reckon I can use an assistant. Somebody to do the cleaning and the scrubbing, make the beds and things like that. Somebody to keep me from feeling lonely at night. A maid of all work, like."

"How does that grab you?" I said to the brunette.

"Ah, shit!" she said, with immense feeling.

"It sounds like a great idea," I said.

"I'll get her a proper uniform," he said enthusiastically. "All black. You know? Black stockings and garters and—"

"I know," I said.

"There's something else I wanted to talk to you about, too," he said.

"I know that, too," I agreed, "but not in here."

We left Moira Stevens locked in her room, and went back to my suite. Hicks made us both a drink, then looked at me with a strictly old-fashioned look on his face.

"You never got no name from DuPlessis," he said. "By the time he came out of that window he had more holes in him than a bleeding fishing net!"

I sat down in an armchair and carefully cradled my drink in both hands. "Consider the situation in Malagai, just before the revolt," I said.

"Fuck that!" he said crisply.

"You're still my employee, Hicks," I said, even more crisply. "So when your master speaks, you're obliged to goddamned well listen!"

"If it's that bleeding important," he snarled.

"The Nkria were in the majority and were the government," I said. "The Imroda were in the minority and were rebellious. They had been building toward an armed revolt for the last couple of years. They never stood a prayer. The Nkria outnumber them, are better fighters, and are also backed by a major power. If it had been allowed to build for another year, when it finally happened it would have been another Biafran situation all over again. But the injection of thirty white mercenaries, and a shipload of modern weapons, persuaded the Imroda they were ready. Then they found the shipment had been sabotaged. The white mercenaries lost heart real fast, and so did the Imroda. The rebellion was put down in four days. It was a joke! The Nkria were so delighted at their absolute superiority, they behaved very generously toward their defeated enemy. They also realized they had to behave a little more circumspectly toward the Imroda, or the same thing would happen all over again in a few years time, and they might not be so lucky then."

Hicks stared at me for a long time without speaking, the white scar on his face pulsating in a regular rhythm.

"Are you trying to tell me," he said finally, "that it was you who sabotaged that bloody shipment?"

"Of course I am," I said.

"Twenty-five of the mercenaries dead," he said. "A lot of the blacks, too!"

"And as Mr. Nkrudu told me," I grunted, "the Imroda leaders were hung, a few women were raped, and the odd child was put to the bayonet. I don't like the thought, either. But if I had let it keep on building to what it would have been a year from now, the Imroda would probably have been totally wiped out, right down to the last woman and child."

He still stared at me for what seemed a long time, then he shook his head slowly. "I don't know about you, mate," he said, "and that's a bloody fact! You realize there's not one bleeding mercenary left now out of the whole bunch?"

"It's a hazardous profession," I admitted. "You probably did the right thing in getting out when you did."

"I'm going out and get stinking bloody drunk," he said.

"Why not?" I said.

"Let me get one thing straight before I go," he said. "You told the Malagaians what you'd done, and that's why this Nkrudu deposited that money for you in the Swiss bank?"

"No," I said bleakly. "I never told them. That's what's worrying the hell out of me right now. Somebody else must have told them, and I have no idea who the hell it was."

"Now I'm going out to get stinking drunk, for sure!" Hicks said, and marched determinedly out of the room.

I took my time about finishing my drink, then started to feel lonely. Then I remembered that company was only in the suite directly across the hallway, so why didn't I join them?

"We thought you'd never get here," Angela said, when I walked into their suite.

"We've waited so long for you, Paul!" Francine pouted her lower lip at me. "We would have been so mad at you if you hadn't come, after we took so much trouble over dressing the right way for the occasion."

They were standing there side by side, totally nude, and making a magnificent contrast in femininity: Angela, with her long blond hair flowing down her back and her white body so richly curved and generously in proportion; Francine, with her close-cropped black hair and lithe brown body that was impossibly slender at the waist, but with two perfectly shaped breasts.

"We thought we should get into training for the yacht," Angela said brightly. "Would you like some champagne?"

"By the way, darling." Francine arched her eyebrows at me. "Just out of curiosity, did you ever hear from a nice black man called Nkrudu?"

"Why do you ask, my love?" I smiled at her vaguely.

"I met him at a party just after I got back from our lovely sea voyage," she said. "I have to admit I was just a little teensy-weensy bit drunk at the time. He was boasting how his government had put down the revolution with almost no bloodshed at all, and I got tired of it so I told him they wouldn't have gotten anywhere without clever you."

"How's that?" I said.

"Darling Paul!" She shook her head quickly. "I saw you that night. I woke up and saw you sneaking out of the cabin, and I remembered you said it was your turn to guard all those dreadful guns down in the hold. So then, a little later, I thought wouldn't it be nice and lovingly sacrificing of me if I went down and kept you company. But when I got down there, I saw what you were doing and I thought you might get mad at me if I disturbed you, so I went back to the cabin."

"And you told Mr. Nkrudu?" I said.

"Of course." She tossed her head. "I told him his government wouldn't still be in power if it hadn't been for your brilliant idea of sabotaging all those guns and things. It was a brilliant idea, wasn't it, Paul?"

"It seemed like it, at the time," I admitted.

More Suspense Thrillers from SIGNET

☐ **FUZZ by Ed McBain.** An 87th Precinct Mystery which involves a homemade bomb, a couple of fun-loving youngsters and an ingenious extortion scheme which add up to big excitement. (#T5151—75¢)

☐ **THE MEPHISTO WALTZ by Fred Mustard Stewart.** A masterpiece in suspense and quiet (the most deadly) horror. Only the strongest will resist its subtly diabolic power. (#Q4643—95¢)

☐ **HAIL, HAIL, THE GANG'S ALL HERE! by Ed McBain.** In this 87th Precinct mystery all of Ed McBain's detectives come together for the first time and they're all kept hopping. Some of the stories are violent, some touching, some ironic, but all are marked by the masterful McBain touch . . . the "gang" has never been better. (#T5063—75¢)

☐ **THE WALTER SYNDROME by Richard Neely.** A psychopathic rapist who calls himself The Executioner terrorizes all New York, as one after another violated and grotesquely mutilated female corpse is found. You are invited to discover the strange and terrible secret of his identity—if your nerves and stomach can take it! "An eerie thriller . . . even the most hardened reader will feel its impact."—*The New York Times* (#Y4766—$1.25)

☐ **THE PAPER DOLLS by L. P. Davies.** This highly acclaimed suspense novel explores the mind of a twelve-year-old English schoolboy possessing extraordinary and potentially evil powers. (#Q4866—95¢)